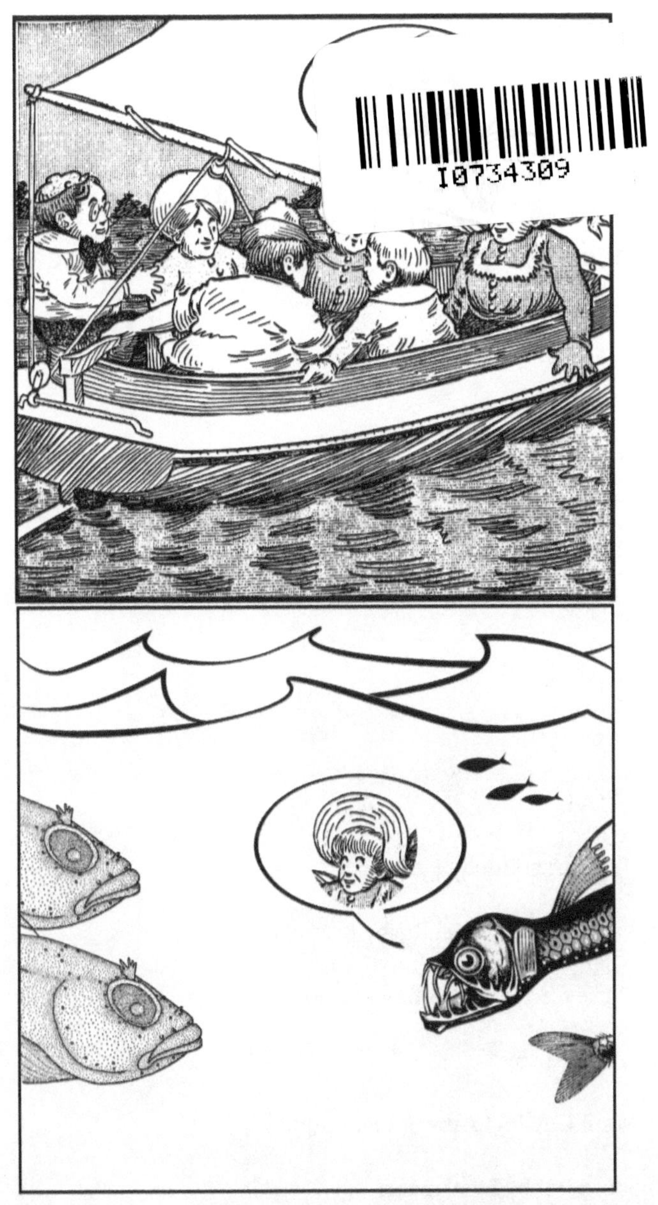

DEEP OVERSTOCK

#4: Nautical Lore
March 2019

NAUTICAL - NAUT LORE

EDITORIAL

EDITOR-IN-CHIEF: Bobby Eversmann

MANAGING EDITORS: Ariel Kusby & Mickey Collins

PROSE: Mickey Collins & Bobby Eversmann

POETRY: Ariel Kusby

SOCIAL MEDIA: Ariel Kusby & Piers Rippey

WEB DESIGN: Bobby Eversmann

INTERIOR DESIGN: Mickey Collins

COVER: Matt Funk

CONTACT: deepoverstock@gmail.com
deepoverstock.com

ON THE SHELVES

Letter from the Editors

Ahoy and avast ye scallywags. This here be Issue 4 of Deep O'. We've explored space, played in fairy tales, and fell in love with some questionable life choices. And it's led to this: Nautical Lore. Just one year ago Deep Overstock was created as an isle in the ocean for lost and marooned souls: booksellers.

There are times, wandering up and down aisles when inspiration hits like a berg on the sea. And you have to answer that call. Dead men may tell no tales, but live booksellers have many things to say. As does the sea. Or any body of water really if you listen closely enough.

In this issue our writers redefine what nautical lore is, everything from selkies to pirates, and whales to selkies, and selkies to pools. Selkies are pretty cute aren't they?

We would like to thank you once again for choosing to pull in Deep Overstock from the murky waters of the shelves. And also to thank everyone who participated in our first cover contest. The winner graces our cover like a beautiful mermaid on the bow, while our runner ups are nestled inside these pages like cannonballs inside a cannon.

But don't worry, because these captains aren't going down with the ship, because the ship isn't going down any time soon. You are all our first mates so stick with around. And look forward to our next issue. It'll be the dreamiest one yet...

Deep Overstock Editors

The Joy-Lord of La Jolla

by Jonathan van Belle

Joymax was an experiment, an Adonis, a demigod.

Eugene, Joymax's father, was wealthy, so Joymax, Eugene's only child, was wealthy. And Eugene's wealth he consecrated to the perfection of his son, as a herald of human perfections to come. Joymax would be raised like John Stuart Mill and Montaigne—by a father's *idée fixe*: "the perfected organic unity of life," Eugene called it. Eugene also called this unity of life, *Le Palais Idéal* or "The Ideal Palace" (a term and dream he took from Ferdinand Cheval). Eugene pushed young Joymax to attain "The Paradisiacal Eye," the eye that sees this world only as a paradise, only joyously.

In addition to the more usual forms of self-enhancement, such as exercise and healthy diet, Eugene's perfectionism also took eccentric forms: one ought to sit in the waves at least once a week for two hours; one ought to hover over the toilet while urinating or defecating, as it is always "an opportunity" to strengthen one's squat; one ought to drink the Bird-of-Paradise flower as a tea every month, steeping its orange sepals and purplish-blue petals for seven minutes exactly; one ought to read Nietzsche every week.

But what if pleasure and displeasure were so tied together that whoever wanted to have as much as possible of one must also have as much as possible of the other—that whoever wanted to "jubilate up to the heavens" would also have to be prepared for "depression unto death"?

So wrote Nietzsche in The Gay Science, and so agreed Eugene. Paradise, Eugene pointed out in the Book of Genesis, is guarded by flaming swords—by a burning, piercing, painful gate. "So God drove out the man," Eugene would recite to Joymax, "and God placed cherubim at the east of the garden of Eden, and a flaming sword which turned every way, to guard the way to the tree of life." Dante, he often added, finds paradise *down through* the inferno.

This was Joymax's childhood and young adulthood—and

Joymax *loved* it.

Joymax loved his beauty, his strength, his intellect, and *his* sunshine, which flooded the white decks and outdoor terraces of his father's seaside mansion in La Jolla, "The Jewel."

Eugene died from bone cancer on a Wednesday. Young Joymax had no "Paradisiacal Eye" for those last months, those bone-pains metastasizing inside his father, pains that need the most morphine, and even then—

It is raw to see others die. It is raw to die. It is raw to love and die. Joymax recalled a line by the Roman playwright Vitus Marinus: *Human, what say you to the nightmare of a perfect god?*

Why *that* line, Joymax wondered.

***

Hodie aperuit nobis clausa porta

It was a Wednesday, one year and seven months after his father's death, when Joymax swam out from La Jolla Cove. With a whisper of Latin—*Hodie aperuit nobis clausa porta*, "Today was opened unto us a closed gate"—our beautiful Joymax pushed out alone, into green-blue waves.

Approximately 2,600 miles away lapped clear waves on Honolulu's shores. Those shores, and no others, would welcome Joymax to land again; Joymax had sworn this to himself.

The year and seven months before had meant to Joymax only preparation for his solitary swim, and for drowning, if it come; and for the ugly shredding and bleeding-out of a shark attack, if it come; and for shock and stroke, if it come.

A wetsuit would be all his protection against 2,600 miles of the cold Pacific. A harness strapped to his torso would tug behind him a wide raft with his supplies: water, dried fruits, Bird-of-Paradise tea, and other staples for raw surviving.

After the 500th mile, Joymax began to talk to the water; his mouth would fill with water, and the water would hum and bubble with his words.

"Do you hear my voice, you deep wilderness?"

After the 1000th mile, Joymax began to sing to the water; his mouth would fill with water, and the water would dance and whirl with his singing.

"We sing to each other, we depths."

Joymax sang to the ocean a song of jubilee.

"I am a ship," he sang, feeling the frigid water as flaming swords. "My passengers, the hopes of those bodies now rotted down, their hopes in the body transfigured, lifted up, saved from destruction, crowned."

After the 2000th mile of his arduous swim, Joymax began to hover over the water.

"I am the aloha spirit," he said to the face of the waters.

"Perfect God," replied the waters, "what say you? What shall we become?"

"Perfect," said the Joy-Lord.

At least
by Monika Kawiak

Stay sharp

Keep the rudder steady

And stay away

From drylands

You will hear voices

But no need to feel fear

It's not your loved ones

Calling you home

It is just the sea

Singing you to sleep

And promising

You will find all answers

To all troubling questions

Laying on its smooth floor

And yes it will be to late

But at least it will be forever

Me Peg

by Michael Calkins

". . . because 'is ear were in the soup! Har, har, har. Ooh, ow! Me peg 'and!"

"Aye, that's right, a 'ook is more usual, only Ol' Sawbones 'ad no 'ooks at the time. Now 'e's got some, but I got so used to the peg, I just kept it.

"Croc took the 'and. Nibbled it off me arm, dainty as you please, while I were napping on the beach. I 'ardly knew 'e'd done it, except me first mate calls out, 'Cap'n, that croc just took your 'and.' And so 'e 'ad, and I even respect 'im for it. Har, har, har. Ooh, ow! Me peg pinkie toe!

"You might not think it, but Ol' Sawbones told me it were important to 'ave the peg to balance me 'ealth, otherwise I were sure to catch the syphilis. Ol' Sawbones is a man of learning, so 'e is, and not a pinch of syphilis 'ave I 'ad.

"Barracuda took the toe. I were dangling me feet in the surf when, silent as a cloud, that thieving fish snatched off me toe. I don't 'old no grudges, though. Let me guard down. Har, har, har. Ooh, ow! Me peg uterus!"

"You 'eard me right. Me peg uterus. Not that I were born with one, you understand. You see, we used to 'ave a gal onboard name of Salty Sal. She weren't much to look at, but she were warm company in a cold 'ammock. One day we were skirmish-ing with Cap'n Grundley and Sal got 'erself between one of 'is cannonballs and meself. It tore right through 'er, rest 'er soul, and 'ad just enough left to dent me gut.

"Ol' Sawbones sewed me up with Sal's uterus inside. 'e said it were too close to me nethers to risk taking it out. Well, I take no chances with me nethers, so in it stayed."

"Aye, that's not a peg. You see, six months later I were floating in me tub when this scoundrel shark gnawed me middle and slurped out Sal's uterus like 'e were 'elping 'imself to seconds at a buffet. Clever boy to find me in me tub. Ol' Sawbones sewed me up (I were near tore in 'alf). 'e said since me nethers 'ad 'ad time to get friendly with Sal's uterus it were fair dangerous to leave them alone so sudden. So 'e plopped in a peg and me nethers 'ave been right as rain, though she's a terror when I 'ave to pee.

"Which I do now, if you'll pardon me. It were a right pleasure speaking with you. Har, har, har. Ooh, ow! Me peg . . .."

Composition

by Benjamin Kessler

A woman with green highlights waves me down on the street and asks if I have thirty seconds to help the whales. I tell her I am sorry that I do not, which is a lie as I am only on my way to Fatburger to meet a friend. As I pass she hands me a brightly-colored pamphlet and a flyer with a link to a website where I can enter my credit card information. In exchange for my donation I can receive my choice between a tote bag and an umbrella.

"Every dollar helps," she says, already in the process of engaging another passerby.

Coming back—two ground beef patties heavy in my belly—I notice that the woman is gone, and in her place sits a beggar with a cardboard sign: it's my birthday, scrawled in shaky permanent marker.

At home I fish the crumpled pamphlet out of my pocket and set it on the bedside table. It uncurls slowly like a fist. There is a long crease across the face of an adult humpback whale, glossy paper cracking white like a tilted mouth.

Before bed I practice my ritual: ensure the stove is off, the doors locked, meat left in the fridge to thaw. While setting my alarm I pick up the pamphlet and unfold it over my lap, if nothing more than to occupy my hands. Inside are graphic photos of whale stomachs cut open, plastic bags slick with bile spilling out on the beach and men in hip waders measuring the dimensions of propellor scars—length, width, depth. More than little disgusted, I clumsily refold the pamphlet and place it back on the nightstand.

I dream of ocean, empty water column, waves cut through with sunlight.

As I crane to silence my alarm I am greeted again with the humpback whale, the crease, though now the corners are also bent, the hinge fold imprecise.

Waking to work I pass another fundraiser, this time a young

"

man with a red cap. He hands me the exact same pamphlet and flyer. This time I stop.

"Yesterday someone gave me this same thing. I looked at it and it was horrifying."

"It's pretty gruesome. They go through a lot, those whales."

"Do you know her, the person who worked here yesterday? She had green hair."

"There's a lot of us, we work in shifts. Sorry."

I'm not going to give him any money, and once he discovers this he loses interest, crossing to the opposite corner and failing to catch the attention of people with earphones in.

Stove checked, doors locked, overnight oats chill in the fridge. I place my new pamphlet, which I kept neatly in my day planner so that it would stay flat, near the old one. I arrange them so they are propped up against the post of the lamp. The blue glow of my cell phone makes the whales seem as though they are in deep, clear water.

I dream again of the ocean, but this time I dive below, discover the dark edges of a sunken ship resting on the seafloor. I can just make out the sea stars pasted to the porthole windows before I am woke by birdsong.

The pamphlet says that in some parts of the world commercial whaling is still practiced, the carcasses pulled from the ocean and processed. At work I spend an hour reading about whale oil online. It was once used in transmission fluid, in lubricants, as a salve for World War One soldiers with trench foot. Before certain legislation it was found in margarine. I could have unknowingly consumed part of a whale on an English muffin.

At the train station there are yet more canvassers, two at every ticket machine. I go down the row and pick up a pamphlet from each. I can barely fit them in my bag, and when I get home I fan them out on my bed.

In my dream I linger outside the sunken ship. When it floated it was a cruise liner, and through the broken doors I see a grand stage. A piano sits on its side, several keys missing. A crab scurries out from beneath the strings. At the far end of the room abandoned roulette wheels are piled in a corner. I think, if I focus, that I can hear something in the distance.

The next morning I don't see any of the whale people on my way to work. Nor do I see them while I walk home.

I linger over the stove, my hands each on a cold burner until the sensation irritates my skin. I do not dream.

Weeks pass and the whale people still don't return. The pamphlets—now curling slightly in the direct sun from the bedroom window—clutter my end table, but I can't bring myself to throw them out. Instead I stuff them into a shoebox, fold them over and wedge them beneath the short table leg, stuff them in my shoes wet from rain.

My sleep is fitful. In my dream I am now high above the ocean, at the height of planes. Birds fly below me, pass through my shadow. The water is simply a silent blue sheet pulled taut against the earth.

I wake up weary, and as I am half-asleep on the train I see through the windscreen a fundraiser positioned on the sidewalk. I get off two stops before my own and run to greet them. I stutter-step around cars, jump over a gentlemen picking through a pile of newspapers.

"I thought you'd gone," I say, gasping for breath.

"Nope! Can you spare a minute to help save the planet? The forests need our help."

There it is. The vest is a different color. They have tablets. There's nothing to hold on to. "You're not with the whales?"

The fundraiser shakes their head no and gives me a sticker that reads #forestranger. I unpeel its paper back and slap it onto a stop sign.

That night I take what remains of the pamphlets and place them in the garbage. For a moment I stand above the can and look at the whale faces speckled with spent coffee grounds, used tissues, and remnants of shredded kitchen sponge.

I am back in the water, but this time I am in the cruise ship's performance hall, sitting in a fine armchair facing an empty stage. I can hear singing, the deep, sinuous whale song that seems to come from all around me. Outside there is nothing. The only thing I think I will remember is the song, that wanting wail that sits in me like water.

<u>Eyepatch</u>

I have a lack of sight

Upon my eye of right

    My lass knows this

    So on my left she'll kiss

Her lover just out of spite

Past ahead
by Monika Kawiak

So it is true what they say

That it is not about

The destination

It is about the water

And the waves

And the wind

And the salt

And there are times

When I am not even sailing

Just drifting

What I know as the past

I carelessly leave behind

Staring watchfully at the horizon

I'm not really curious

About the future

Cause at the end

It always turns out

The same

As the past

The Hammish Sisters

by Desmond Everest Fuller

Before the Hammish sisters disappeared, none of us said the word Selkie. It was a word that seemed old even in the twentieth century, our grandfathers' grandfathers' word. Age was heavy in it, like the rusted schooner anchor from the 1700's that's in front of town hall. By this time, we weren't young anymore ourselves; old words didn't scare us so much as bring about wistful sadness. Selkie. Old but fleeting, as ephemeral as fog in a dream.

In first grade, our class had to draw our family portraits. All swirls of crayon mess, arms and hands too big, dogs and houses too small. Mera and Shawna Hammish drew theirs together, twin mops of black hair swirling together above the sheaf of construction paper. Their five-year-old scribbles showed their mother waving neck deep in the ocean while they stood with their father on the beach. we all laughed. Their mother was drawn as a seal.

The Hammish sisters lived with their dad Tom off the north end of Setters Cove in a double-wide that took the wind all day off the water. Tom had a small dock of his own where he put in his fishing boat. No one believed the stories of him finding the sisters' mother in his fishing nets. But older people did say the wind blew stronger around the Hammish house. The rope securing Tom's boat had to be thicker than any other fisherman in town as the current and errant breezes tugged at his hull like she had tugged his arm towards the breakers that last night.

He nearly drowned swimming after her, searching for her among the waves. Jason Cup's dad was one of the EMTs who sat with Tom in the back of an ambulance, a couple space blankets draped around his sagging shoulders. They drove Tom home, up the winding track to the end of land and his house with two small shapes cut out of yellow light in the front door waiting for him.

He couldn't say she was dead, he muttered, rocking like a buoy between the two EMTs. But she was gone and wasn't coming back. He wouldn't have let her go. He'd of locked her in the house if he thought he could keep her. Tom claimed to have taught her to speak. He said, he taught her the words for wind, bread and fire, for warm, for eyes and lips.

Everyone chalked Tom's ravings up to grief. Our parents said things like it was a shame, those girls growing up without a mother. Jessica Dole's mom encountered Tom at Jan's groceries told him, right there in the dairy aisle, that his wife was in a better place. Tom shot her a look laced with profound bitterness and asked Mrs. Dole why, if it was so much better, wasn't she wasn't in more of a hurry to get there.

Years pasted with the advancing and receding of a thousand tides. At Sixteen, Mera and Shawna Hammish had sat with us through most of school, all of us moving up through the same cramped classrooms as our parents and siblings had before us. They were the stars of the school swim team, and trained every morning in the low tide, zippering parallel the shore, waves crashing over them moving up and down the beach, staying close in the shallow water. Though it was hard to call what they did training. They swam like they were born to it, with a beguiling ease. In the pool, with no waves to drag against them, their lithe bodies seemed to fly, their arms and legs scarcely seeming to move.

Their father, Tom, came to every swim meet and clapped quietly with us all at his daughters' every victory. Even as he'd become otherwise withdrawn and hermetic, he would brave the world to support his daughters. With each year that passed, he watched them with more melancholy as they grew and seemingly thrived almost more in the water than on land.

To say the Hammish girls were beautiful was to prove the failure of words. Their long pillared legs and thick ironwood hair set off an ache in the wood of every boy, and many a girl's teeth and bones. It was a feeling that left us all empty and small, like they could see our pining thoughts. Looking around at ourselves, we couldn't think of anyone who could date either of them.

Lying on our backs on a trampoline in Jenny McVee or Ty Reeve's yard, we'd pair ourselves and everyone we knew in funny and cruel combinations. We laughed in the dark as the trampoline sagged, dumping us all together in the middle.

Some of us secretly paired ourselves with the foot that hooked over our own, or the shoulder that rose two bodies away. We'd laugh and crossed our fingers that something, anything might happen for us. The game would end abruptly at the mention of the Hammish Sisters, and dreams would be fevered with their dark dark eyes and long black hair, the fragile pellucid quality of their skin.

We saw more than one father's gaze linger and follow the sisters along the length of the swimming pool. Fishermen and Coastguards who might have secretly believed Tom Hammish's tales of pulling forth a beautiful woman from the sea. We grew up watching our fathers' boats blink off the dark horizon, returning late each night with salt in their beards and kelp in their nets. The years cut through them like cream, and fostered a quiet desperation for something that would take their breath away.

By the time we were juniors at Setter's High, only Margaret Denbell had been to the Hammish house in years. Tom was her mother's cousin, and she and Margaret checked on Tom and the girls regularly. One night a howler wrapped the house in black rain and a banshee wind that picked up bits of sand and gravel. Margaret and her mother bedded down in the living room rather than drive back to town. She told us she woke in the night to use the bathroom, tiptoeing down the hall. Passing the sister's door, she swore she heard them singing. Twin voices rose and fell with the rushing wind, like the echo of each other, like the sound that lives in a seashell.

As Margaret told it, she went back to burrow under the covers on the couch, too spooked to sleep. Sometime in the unseen hours, she heard them. Shawna and Mera's shadows passed through the living room, quietly slipping out the door. Margaret could never say why she wrapped herself in her mom's coat and followed the sisters out of the house. The wind-whipped sand stung her cheeks, and she could scarcely see the path down to the beach. She followed the singing that broke and fluttered in the storm, leading her down to the edge of the water. There she caught glimpses of two pale bodies rising from the waves surrounded by dark shapes like round polished stones, like the bobbing heads of seals.

As Shawna and Mera approached eighteen, Tom Hammish

became more reclusive, only coming into town for essential groceries, to watch his daughters' swim meets, and to play Keno. He stood watching the flurry of tiny plastic numbered balls flying in the glass globe on the counter of the tavern when Harry Schmidt asked if the girls were nervous about the regional swim meet. Without glancing away from the Keno balls, Tom muttered that soon they would leave him too. Eventually everything returned to the water.

It's been years now since anyone saw the Hammish sisters. Tom Hammish passed away and his little house has stood empty and quiet out at the end of the land, slowing breaking against the wind.

Most of us moved away from Setter's cove, found lives in swaths of the world that didn't break against the tide and rippling sea foam. Those who stayed took on fishing with our fathers. We watch our town slowly fade, every year fewer boats mooring in the harbor. Our joints have began to ache against the hauling of nets. Salt has worked its way into the creases in our skin, and the sea whispers to us late at night in awful dreams.

The old fishermen who remember Shawna and Mera Hammish called the sisters dark ones: quiet in everything they did, kind but distant with everyone. Those of us who remember, imagine one day a fisherman or woman will bring home a quiet stranger who's beauty makes us want to cry, and we'll remember the Hammish Sisters. In their eyes swam a darkness that you could only hear out your window at night as the waves moved and shuffled the edge of the land beneath them under the moon, grinding away at stone and earth, whispering over your dreams that it would get you too one day your life would be returned to the calm hiss of the tide moving in and out forever.

A Sea Shanty for Sandy

by Mickey Collins

I had a woman whose name was Sandy
Around the house she was quite handy.
I was called out to sea, for work you see,
Had a calling for fish, just before tea,

Sandy come back, to me
Sandy share your heart, with me

But a storm was a-brewin' on my port side,
And out on the ocean, nowhere to hide,
I took it head on, but it was an error,
I knocked my head, and when I breathed air,

Sandy come back, to me
Sandy share your heart, with me

A mermaid I saw, the prettiest thing
Her song she sang, my ears did ring
Frozen, I was, by her magical powers
While all I thought of was Sandy's flowers

Sandy come back, to me
Sandy share your heart, with me

This witch of the sea, she stole my heart
I wished I could return to before my depart
But when I made my way back home,
My Sandy--my love--thought I did roam

Sandy come back, to me
Sandy share your heart, with me

She thought I diseased
Something not right, below my knees
Without a heart, I could not fight her,
E'en though I never lost sight of her

Sandy come back, to me

Sandy share your heart, with me

So heed this warning,
Before you end up in mourning
Brothers, leave your hearts with your ladies
Else you be cast down into Hades

Sandy come back, to me
Sandy share your heart, with me

Keep a locket of your loved one near your chest
Remind yourself it's for the best
For now I go from port to port
Stealing hearts of every sort

Sandy come back, to me
Sandy share your heart, with me

For no lady will ever marry this guy
Whose body has sores, no lie
For upon the might sea
I caught an STD
A horrible case of sea-philis

Sandy come back, to me
Sandy share your heart, with me

 Nautilus Girl - Sarah McLeod-Martinez

Our House

by Alec Ballweg

You do not notice it at first. Until you hear the lethargic stirring of a shallow puddle on your way to the kitchen. You look down to find your feet covered in water. It slips between your toes and dances through your arches in the absence of your movement. You think nothing of this: overspill from a water glass or the place where she paused, naked, dripping and absent- minded, on her way from the shower.

She calls to you from the other room and you join her on the couch, fitting yourself to her. Half watching the TV, she kisses you, her hair tickling your nose as she turns. You do not ask about the puddle on the floor. You've forgotten it.

****

It is months now and the water is up to your ankles. It tugs at you, pushing and pulling in a tide you do not understand. You do not know how long it has been like this and you do not ask but the skin at your calves has begun to redden and dry.

Walking around the house, you do not notice the shushing of it against the furniture and the walls. You do not feel it on your legs, but inside of you. The ebbs and flows are in your lungs and the foam rises, pulling itself up your throat. Breathing is heavy and crooked, but you've become used to this, too.

You say nothing but you see it on her, too, the chafing at the ankles, the rot in her steps. You feel the waves in each breath you take and you assume they are in hers, too. She does not tell you, but you think you can taste the salt on her breath. Each time she touches you, you can feel the rising and rippling within. Together, you feel it surge and you wade.

****

It has clawed past your knees, now. You've watched the waterlines rise on the walls and inside of you and you mark the days in these changes. There is no foam anymore. The water is steady and dark and no longer crashes against the walls of your lungs. It holds and you can feel the brine settling instead.

Yesterday, you found her sitting on the kitchen counter drinking a glass of orange juice. She flicked her legs back and forth, dragging her toes across it like a sunbather off a dock. You felt the water rise within yourself and it filled you until you were drowning on your feet. She took a sip and continued tracing lazy patterns with her toes. It was only when the ripples reached you that she looked up.

The glass dropped from her hand and sank, coloring the water, orange fingers reaching their way across the room toward you. You do not know what she saw in you. She said nothing. But that silence howled. You took an apple and left. The water rocked back and forth against the cabinets in your wake and this, too, screamed.

****

There is a storm in your living room today. The waves crash against the windows and walls and your chest. They are rapid and angry and you fear the desperate rise and fall will pull you out with them. Soon enough, your lungs are full and it comes spilling out of you, punching, pushing, rushing for her.

She stands in the middle of it all. You cannot see her but you know, somewhere in the heaving and the spinning and the cracking, she is there. The eye of the storm.

You yell and feel it tear from inside but it breaks before it reaches her. The remains of it patter against the windows like a summer rain and the sound of it quells the waves inside of you. You feel the thunder recede and it slows to a low tide, gentle and warm.

She emerges, windblown and soaked, and she wades to you. The water is up to her chest but she does not fight with it. It moves and fits to her the way the world always has and that is when you realize that the water is yours.

She holds you and says nothing and she feels like the water. But different. She is warm and still and clear and there is no salt on her. She holds you and, for a moment, you're still inside.

****

The water is up to your neck and, some days, it feels like

fingers around your throat. It lives, happy and at home, in your chest and outside. You have gotten used to this. You do not notice the smell of salt anymore. You have forgotten what it is to be dry.

Sometimes, the sky darkens and the waves crash over your head and it is all you can do to breathe. The wind howls and it takes you awhile to realize, to remember, that this comes from you. You wonder what will happen when the house fills all the way. When there is nothing but water.

She is shorter than you and the water is to her mouth. She swims, now. Treading water is easier than walking. Her ripples reach you, gentle and soft, but they shake the world inside.

Your feet rest, pruned, on the bathroom tile and you watch her tread water in the bedroom. You cannot see her hands or feet in the dark water, but you can feel the rhythm of them. Back and forth. Back and forth. Slower each time. And it is now, watching the curtains and the water sway like seaweed, that you know that this is your water. It always has been. And it is here, listening to the tide in your chest and seeing the rising rot on the walls, that you realize she has been awash and drowning all this time.

You put your toothbrush back in the jar beside the sink and, though you can still touch, you swim to her. You say nothing for a moment, letting the waves within and without crash together until they are the same. She does not say anything either because she knows.

One more stroke and you say it. It does not dance on your tongue, but rushes from you, flowing out to sea.

"Okay."

And on the end quotation, the water drains from the house, rushing, pulling, dragging itself away. It drops you both to the floor and leaves nothing but the damp and the salt and the tidelines on the walls. The water inside you remains, but it is yours and you know this and it cannot drown you.

<u>Peg Leg</u>

There once was a captain named Stark

Though Eileen was her nom de lark

She limped, she waddled

Cause in the sea she paddled

With a great white shark in the dark

The Cod and the Whale

by AJD

The deck pitches in a slow roll with the swells, but worse is an irregular jolting motion which induces a drunken stumble gait. It is night, raining hard, and windy. There is a constant roar from the storm and the workings of the deck. Sailors run to and fro with jet fuel and bombs, toolboxes and short little light sticks — like those cheap Star Wars light saber toys, but shorter — for guiding jets into their parking spots.

My cod has landed and we're parked aft of the island. I trail after someone who seems to be guiding the passengers with a pale yellow light stick. He has on a green jersey and I begin to wonder if we're following the right guy. F-14s and A-7s are prepping to launch up ahead, thick steel cables snap loudly to the side, and all around us the deck is being frantically cleared for what looks like an emergency recovery drill.

The group splits up. A few sailors go into different doors. Others wander away to service various planes and equipment. If there was a group of passengers being led to safety, I've lost them. Feeling abandoned and exposed, I decide to go to the side of the island where passengers are normally taken, in my limited experience.

I'm carrying thirty pounds of flight gear in one hand and my sea bag in the other, clumsily navigating parked deck tractors. Hot oil fumes from the hydraulics mixes with the pervasive JP-5 to burn my eyes and sinuses. Through my tears, and the wind and spray, I can see no visible demarcation of the deck's edge, normally a 90-foot drop, now rising and setting to the storm.

A Corsair launches with a roar, the fire of the engines momentarily lighting up the flight deck with harsh light and shadow. I stumble, scrape my hands and a knee on the non-skid, then sprawl forward across some metal tubes I fear might be sidewinders — an act which could make me infamous, the cause of the next Forrestal disaster. A deck monkey barks at me from behind while a hatch opens dead ahead. I go in, momentarily knocking into a group of aircrew coming out.

The light is red and feeble in the corridor. I push into a space lit by a lone fluorescent tube on the bulkhead. Amazingly it is the right place. I see a few of the other passengers seated on folding chairs. No one notices me or talks to me. The cod airdales run in and out of the room. They won't answer any questions, nor look at our orders.

No one from my squadron is there to pick me up like they should be. I scan the room for a boat phone book to call them, but of course they wouldn't be in it as they're only t-a-d to the ship. And since I'm only t-a-d to them, I'm less than nothing to most people onboard. I feel totally insignificant and miserable.

I'm hot already, as the room is crowded and starting to steam. I pull off my watch cap and tug at my woven undergarments. It was cold on the cod — not as cold as the whale, but still, glad to have them. Then, and especially in the weeks to come at eight miles up, they're wonderful. Not now, though.

I'll hit the head in a minute and ditch the thermals — in a minute, though. I lean back against a steel column and close my eyes against the sweat and nausea, the exhaustion and anxieties of travel. I start to drift off, speculating about nuclear steam, when, at a sudden command, all the stragglers from the transport are rounded up and shoved into the dim corridor.

The hatch closes amid our confused protest. Someone mentions g-q, but my mind draws a blank on the meaning of this particular military acronym. Right away we see people pouring up the ladder and into the short passageway. We huddle against the bulkhead to let them by. The third person to pass, doesn't, but stops above me. It's too dark for me to make him out clearly.

He addresses me by name and says I'm needed for the next whale launch. I need to get up there, asap, he says. Happily, I remember that I can't get up there asap for the next whale launch because I have no parachute harness; this is to be issued to me by the rigger.

The dark silhouette holds still for a moment, then gestures sharply. He tells me to GET One from the rigger, ASAP! I tell him I don't know how to get to the squad shack. He starts to gives me some questionable directions, stops, then shouts in my face: "YOU know how to get to the FUCKING squad shack, GODDAMN YOU!"

At this, he's off.

And so am I, in the opposite direction. The force of his last statement is such that it convinces me that I do indeed know how to get to the squad shack. There are more than 5,000 people on this ship and every nook and cranny is somebody's office, repair shack, or sleeping space. I'm not thinking of this when I go down the first few ladders.

He said the quickest way would be through the cafeteria, which complies with my general knowledge of where they usually put us. The mess is always down about four or five decks. The ladders rarely go straight down for more than a couple decks, so I'm out and into other passageways, dimly lit from red and orange lights above the hatches.

After dead-ending twice, I decide to pass through some dark berths. At first, I perceive them as unpopulated, but soon I'm getting shoved around in the dark. I feel very bad. I'm lost, and my squadron is expecting me to fly on some sort of mission. Even if I could find my way, I'm sick at the thought of having to crawl into the belly of that decrepit old jet, the whale, to get launched into a night like this. And that g-q thing is nagging at me.

I find an exit to another corridor, then down one more deck to the blue cafeteria floor. There is tape stretched across the hatchway. I can't cross it. I could, actually, but I'm quite timid about breaking somebody's rules here — even though it's probably just some lowly E-1s buffing the floor. It's just that the light down there is also red, like the passageways, not bright white like the cafeteria is usually lit.

So I'm back up the stairs, but now I can't get out of the stairwell. The hatches are all secured. I go up and up and up until I'm sure I must be inside the island, above the flight deck. I put my bags down frequently as I am exhausted. I finally find an open hatch.

As I'm entering another corridor, I remember.

G-Q. General Quarters. Like Red Alert on Star Trek.

Everyone is supposed to be at their battle stations, but I don't know where mine is. I run quickly towards what I think is the center of the ship, but am soon forced to open a hatch, since all of them are closed now, at least all the ones I can see.

My sea bag gets stuck and I can't get through. I feel exposed in the open corridor, panicked at the possibility of Marines charging past, gleefully beating the hell out of anyone in their way, as they are licensed to do during G-Q.

I force in the bag and step into another berthing area. My appearance seems to pass unnoticed as everything stays still and quiet, even as I re-secure the hatch. I emerge from a curtain into the tv room. It is dark, except for the blue-green light of the cathode rays shooting out from the box. The sound is down and still no one is talking. Everyone seems frozen still, except for someone standing next to the tv. His hand moves in slow motion. On the closed circuit flight deck channel I can clearly see the whale being readied to launch. The image goes to static then flicks onto an old WWII movie.

I don't know why, but I've had enough. I can't stand it in this room another second. I pull back a different curtain to the main sleeping area and pass into endless rows of triple-stacked bunk beds. Dim bulbs protrude from the padded ceiling. They shower the room with a red haze. I have my sea bag in front of me and my flight bag behind me. I walk slowly, cautiously. I hear occasional whimpering from behind the curtained bunks.

I wonder if there really is a G-Q going on. The somnambulist behavior of the seamen in here does not seem indicative. And I never heard anyone actually say that there was a G-Q. I just heard it mentioned. Such uneasy ambiguity is a familiar sensation, and dismaying.

I set down my bags as my arms are killing me.

There probably isn't a g-q. I just need to calm down. I slouch against a metal beam wrapped in foam and slide, remembering how my "battle station" is sometimes my bunk on aircraft carriers, since there is so little room. With a cringe of self-loathing, I recall how I crept in and cowered there during the first few drills — as much from a feeling of frustrated rage vaguely directed at the edifice of stupidity that is the military, as from any fear that I might drown, forgotten in my bed.

I recline and stretch my legs outward, beneath the floor panel, into an impossible tangle of wiring. Far above some scattered puffy clouds, shadowing a moonlit sea, the jet's windows are frosty against a deep black night. I'm in the whale. The battery of electronic equipment in front of me, which I am supposed to be operating, lies dormant, unlit. I am fast asleep, oblivious, even as all hell starts to break loose inside the cramped fuselage.

I wake up with a start and try to get my bearings. Is that right? The whale was ready to launch and I'm not there? And a G-Q?

Wait, I think. Of course it's real! I was just in the ready room when we heard that there was a p-t boat a couple hundred yards off port. We were running through the ship, D and I. Shit! I've got to be on that plane or they'll have my ass.

No, that's not what happened. I just landed on this boat a half hour ago.

It's all blurring together. I pick up my bags. I feel very nauseated and disoriented. Am I drunk? Hungover? Sick with ear infections, antibiotics, decongestants, pain killers? Scared shitless? I'm sure of only the last, but the rest are true too. They all happen.

There's a down hatch ahead which I recognize. I stumble forward.

This is always here and it always ends like this.

The lid is held by chains to the bulkhead at a 60-degree angle. I approach and look inside. Far below, light sticks scratch out precise directions until the tiny diorama is lost in a cloudy mist. The ladder is very long, but a humming warmth emanates from the depths. I know this is a dream, and I've known it all along. I know that the p-t boat turns out to be a spy trawler, that I get on the whale and help kill some people, that we're spiraling down for a trap that goes sideways, that part of me stays below.

—the end

<u>Hook</u>

It's not easy having a hook for a hand

And getting kicked out of your ska band

Though songs I did write

The notes were a fright

And so I was left in neck-deep in the sand

Sailing Jupiter

by Ben Talley

Jupiter was a pinprick in the night sky. Above the Moon and to the right, easily mistakable for a distant star. But Marsh knows where to look. They'd been hoping for a glimpse of Europa, soon to be their new home, but Jupiter's fledgling moon was lost in the reflecting glow of Earth's moon, shining bright and full.

"Is it still up there?" asked Marsh's Father, emerging from the sailboat's small cabin with a fresh six-pack.

"Hard to tell with this old thing," said Marsh.

The telescope Marsh was using was their Father's, a seemingly immortal device that had been Frankensteined by various compatible pieces over the years, giving it a half-rusty/half-shiny new complexion.

"Well, if it ain't, your Uncle's not gonna be too happy when I tell him we're keepin' the boat." Father handed Marsh a beer and they cracked it open, the sharp sound of snapping metal distinct against the soft rocking of the ocean water around them.

Father's boat was a source of pride for the old sailor. He had always been more comfortable on water than on land, living his entire adult life on various houseboats as he bounced around the country and its eclectic lakes and ports, working as a crewman on numerous fishing vessels and freight liners. In his spare time he sailed. Working, sleeping, playing, loving, raising a family. He did it all on the water. But when Marsh's Mother got sick, when she was being treated, when the treatments failed, when they had to let her go, that had all been on land. In the two years that followed Father built a sailboat, pouring years of pain and loss and anger into a vessel of his own creation. Victory's Wing he named her, after Marsh's Mother, Victoria. When it was complete, waxed and finished and ready to fly, Father boarded the boat and rarely set foot on land again.

Too bad he couldn't take it with him to Europa, what with the planet being mostly water and ice. He imagined exploring those seas like the old North Pole expeditions centuries back. Nothing but your wits and determination to guide you. The colony ship was packing tight and light, however, leaving no room for personal belongings, least of which a sailboat.

"So we'll build a new one," said Marsh when he expressed his concerns.

Like their Father, Marsh was looking for a new start, and they didn't get newer than the Europa colony. Opportunity on Earth was dwindling for its youth, just as the planet itself, and the unrelenting sense of adventure and expedition that came with being raised on the water was something that plagued Marsh in a world that prided and praised structure and stability. More than that, though, Marsh was First Mate to Father's Captain. He taught them how to sail while they were learning to crawl, to walk, to speak. As long as they were together neither sailed alone, and as far as Marsh was concerned that included the stars.

"Build a new what?" asked Father.

"A new sailboat."

Father scoffed, but Marsh was serious.

"You said it yourself, Europa's mostly water," they said, "You're telling me you don't wanna be the first person to sail on another planet? I say we cut our teeth on Europa, the whole planet's smaller than the Pacific, and then we take on the big one."

"Big one?"

"Jupiter."

Father chuckled. "You never did mind sailing straight into a storm."

Father's smirk slowly faded as he looked up towards the sky and contemplated the notion.

"What would we build it out of?"

From there Marsh knew they had their Father convinced. He looked at his child to see them smiling. He could already see the gears turning in the engineer's mind.

As Marsh stood there thinking, Father lifted his chin and took a deep breath.

"Do you think the salt will smell the same?" he asked.

"It's possible."

"I hope it does." He took another deep breath with closed eyes, as if he was trying to preserve the scent in his memory.

Neither of them spoke for the rest of the night. Instead they sat portside of the aging sailboat, absorbing the scene surrounding them. The purity of the silence. The cool warmth of the air. The feathering breeze. During this time the water became so still that the cloudless, star-speckled sky was reflected upon it, the mirrored horizon giving them the impression of sailing eternity.

In two months, and for the next three years, they would take flight for real.

*

Jupiter was a cathedral ceiling painted by Time. It stretched across the sky, from ear to ear, bathing its moon in a warm crimson glow. Europa, the cathedral, sprouted mighty pillars and mountain crests of ice that seemed to hold Jupiter in place. When the ruby giant was full the seas that cradled and flowed beneath the arctic lands of the moon turned tumult, flailing and dancing in worship to the mother god that gave it life, shaped it in orbit alongside its many brother and sister moons. The gleeful rioting of the congregation cracked the cathedral walls, dividing the house in some places and merging them in others. For the recently settled Europans there was little to fear, having established their home on the icy continent at the moon's south pole, where the land was thick and the worship more subdued.

Still, landing on the moon presented its own difficulties. The mission charters had not predicted exactly how violent the sub-oceans would turn and thus how drastically the lands would shift. As they were preparing to touch down in an arctic valley ridged by a ring of icy mountains a tectonic shift occurred, forcefully enough to shift the mountains themselves. One of them collided with the titanic vessel upon its descent, forcing the pilots to make an emergency crash landing at the base of the opposite ridge, wherein an avalanche buried the craft's back third.

There was miraculously no loss of life except that concerning the ship itself. The propulsion systems and the entirety of the engine room were encompassed in several hundred tons of ice.

Marsh and the rest of the engineering crew narrowly escaped the same fate.

Over the next several months while the colony unpacked and erected their sprawling new home, the leaders debated the merits, and possibility, of recovering the ship. By the time they realized they did not have the resources to pull off such a feat while their colony was still so young, Marsh had drawn the blueprints for theirs and Father's new ship. Out of the scraps of the vessel that brought them to their new home, the ship in which they sailed the stars, Victory's Wing II was constructed.

The project took over a decade to complete. In what little spare time they had each day Marsh and their Father ventured into the dilapidated engine room and carefully removed sections of metal, insulated carbon meshing, lengths of piping, and other materials that were otherwise useless to the quickly thriving settlement. They then assembled the materials and deconstructed, warped, and welded the pieces together to create the body of the ship, and used the carbon meshing as a sail. Luckily for them the winds on Europa were mightier than Earth's, forceful enough to drag and lift the thicker, heavier sail.

Victoria's Wing II sailed for many years across the jagged saltwater lakes and ever-shifting rivers of Europa's surface, with Marsh taking on the role of Captain in the new world and Father of First Mate. Together they charted the more stable regions of the moon within their reach, accounting for the areas that were perpetually in flux. It became their jobs, their contributions to the community to draw maps of the areas they covered, and over time they had mapped out the entire southern hemisphere. They had planned to attempt crossing the most treacherous waters of the equator to enter the northern hemisphere, an adventure the more headstrong and daring Marsh longed for, but as time went on Father became older and less able to assist. The frigid air, relentless wind thrust, and tiring work of chipping ice off the ship's hull took its toll on the man, though he'd never admit it. Whenever the pains of age threatened to overcome him, he would simply take a whiff of the salty air and be reminded of home.

One day they were out on a leisurely drift about the river that snaked through their home valley and circled the mountain range surrounding it, drinking "Jovian home brew" provided by a neighbor and watching Jupiter's slow rise on the horizon.

Sunlight reflecting off the sliver in view lit up their world with a coral glow.

"Sunrise never quite looked like this back on Earth, did it?" asked Father.

"Understatement of the year," said Marsh, sipping their brew.

"Winds are a lot stronger up there. Lot stronger," said Father, glancing around at the boat. "Gonna need a thicker hull. Don't know what you're gonna use for the sail, winds'll tear right through anything thicker than steel. Hell, they might tear through steel."

"I've got a few ideas. We'll figure something out."

Father sighed, turning his eyes back up toward the giant.

"You know I can't come with you."

"I know you think you can't."

"Marsh, I'm old. I can barely walk the length of this boat anymore without having to catch my breath. I can't go ridin' a hurricane with you. 'Sides, you're more competent of a captain than I ever was. Much more."

"Dad, forget it. You're coming with me. You never even have to leave the cabin."

"Marsh—"

"We're a team. End of story."

Father looked at Marsh with proud eyes. He knew Jupiter was next for his child, but it was not going to be last. He only wished he could be around to see it.

*

Jupiter is an ocean. Its rose dusted winds rushing as rivers pressed against one another, generating titanic storms that could shake the foundations of Mt. Olympus. Its depths plunge towards eternity, its horizon wider than the breadth of stars. Its surface radiates with the color palette of the most brilliant sunset painted skies. If Earth's sea floor is Davy Jones' Locker, then

Jupiter's heights are the sailor's Valhalla. And Marsh had been knocking on the Great Hall's doors for days.

Victoria's Wing III, its previous incarnation repurposed with a Samson-strength hull, was shaped like a raindrop turned on its side. It rode an amber vortex around the circumference of the lower half of the planet with one single fin sprouting up and at an angle, a steel alloy sail turning the boat ever so slightly towards what Marsh hoped would eventually be the vortex's barrier.

They were nestled within the cramped cabin of the ship, lying underneath the protruding sail and tightening bolts loosened by the sheer tug of the wind from the outside. A hurricane roar filled the boat with such omnipresence since they entered Jupiter's atmosphere that when all fell silent they were deaf to the change for several moments. In fact it wasn't the sound at all that tipped them off, but the relaxation of the ship itself. The vibrations of the vessel that Marsh hadn't even realized they'd gotten used to ceased entirely, as if the boat had slipped into a frictionless environment.

Excitedly, Marsh donned their wind-resistant coat and goggles, tied the carbon fiber rope that was anchored to the cabin's floor around their waist, and climbed the central ladder towards the roof of the boat. They twisted the wheel, pushed open the hatch, and were awestruck by the first Jovian vista they could witness with their own eyes.

They were drifting within a clear atmospheric pocket a mile wide between two of Jupiter's mighty vortices. On either side of Marsh towered walls of the planet's trademark red winds, reaching heights that dwarfed entire moons and plunging farther down than Hades. But what struck Marsh with awe and fear and exhilaration was what lied ahead.

Victoria's Wing III's destination was a once distant red blemish seen through a telescope, a bloodshot eye on the godlike face of Jupiter, a centuries old storm that could swallow Earth twice and still have room for more. The Great Red Spot. It boiled and toiled and raged like the Kraken of sailor myth, waiting to drag down any who dared enter its sacred waters.

Marsh smiled.

They climbed back down into the cabin and sealed the hatch.

They adjusted the sail to send the boat back towards the border of one of the vortices that would eventually skirt around the Storm, riding its razor's edge all the way down. Marsh kept an iron grip on the sail's lever, using all their strength not to slip and send the boat tumbling back into the vortex. Sweat coated their skin and soaked their clothes. The Storm's beastlike roar was deafening, a physical presence that enveloped Marsh inside and out. When it was almost too loud to bear, Marsh guessed they were close enough. With a tremendous shift of weight they twisted the lever and thus the sail, bouncing the boat off the vortex wall and straight into the Storm.

In the breath of a second between winds Marsh moved to a bucket seat in the cabin's corner and strapped in.

The next several moments Marsh could only later describe as trying to ride a furious bull strapped to a rickety roller coaster during the San Andreas Quake. While their entire world shook the only thought that crossed Marsh's mind was the look their Father would have on his face if he were there with them. "You never did mind sailing straight into a storm," he'd shout.

Then unexpectedly it was over. The silence that followed was pure. Marsh couldn't help but think they might be dead and the rest of their senses hadn't caught up yet. They rested a moment, waiting for a sudden shift back to fury, but it never came. Carefully, Marsh unbuckled their seatbelt, climbed the ladder, and opened the hatch.

They stood upon the surface of Victoria's Wing III and witnessed wonder.

They were in the Eye of the Storm. The slightest of breezes was all that passed them by in the epic breadth, raising the hairs on their arms and neck. Surrounding them at a quiet distance was the churning, cherry red rage of the Storm.

Marsh closed their eyes, took a deep breath, and swore they could almost smell salt.

AQUA: poems from the sea
by Timothy Arliss O'Brien

<u>The fishing incident</u>

An oath taken at dawn

In light of the bright sun
cascading Out of the ocean

An oath to tell no one

Not even thy self

A secret that shall die at sea

And stay at sea

The lifeless wet body

Slumped over the bow of the boat

Slippery and wet into the black abyss.

Half man, half fish.

He had stopped breathing seven minutes after being pulled in
with the net.

Seven minutes of pure bliss, with the most beautiful creature I
have laid eyes upon.

An oath at a funeral,

happening too soon.

The adventure of the ice cave

The ship left port all too late at dusk.
Sailing 36 km due north for the ice fishing spot.

I had traced the location of a lore based deep ice cave only half
an hour's journey west from the popular ice fishing spot.

Legend had it that contained within was a crown, that when
worn would bestow the powers of weather. The ability to cause
storm and tempest, or with the right planning, paradise. Crops
watered properly, and fair weather for all.

Halfway to the fishing spot a thick blizzard started falling
straight down, as if someone was trying to prevent our journey.

We reached the fishing spot extremely later than anticipated,
but in one piece.

The hike for me was effortless as I had been preparing for a
decade, snowshoeing at every chance.

The old manuscript left to me by my grandfather at age nine de-
noted that the stairwell would be located between two bastions
of ice. And they would triangulate with the highest peak into a
perfect isosceles triangle.

I reached the two pinnacles, walked straight between them and
started digging.

It took me ten minutes to hit stone, all too soon for the amount
of snowfall. The stone was the first step and soon I had dug out
ten.

After the fifteenth step my way was paved with crystalline walls
of ice and frigid air.

I soon lost contact with time and seemed to fly down the stairs
faster and faster.

After an indeterminate amount of time I realized I was sur-
rounded by a glow and the ice was melting. I started pressing

against the walls and soon they were collapsing away revealing a large ice cavern, fathoms deep and wide.

Molten lava ran like rivers deep below me, as skyscraper sized stalactites dripped into the smoldering earth.

I could see a raised part of the earth with a crafted pedestal of ice jettisoning upward. I peeked around the corner of the ledge I sat on and was horrified at what I saw.

Frozen little creatures covered in feathers bustled around the ice pedestal carving and polishing it. A huge ice sculpture of a man rose out of the pedestal. Atop his head was a golden crown, encrusted with sapphires and rubies.

At that exact moment the earth started to rumble and a deep voice called out, "Who tresspasess here? Leave my cavern at once!"

I could hear the small creatures squawking and scurrying about, looking for me, I presumed.

Running upward on melting ice stairs that had previously been stone proved to be a challenge. Although I did gain about fifteen steps up before slipping and striking my head against the wet melting ice wall.

I was told upon waking, six months later, that I was found clawing at the snow four days after our ship's departure. No sign of hypothermia, muttering to myself about becoming king.

Red Dawn

Black sky to blue.
Oblivion and peace of mind.

But alas, the crimson clouds warn of fright.

Soon enough, the tempest looms.

The destructive storm terrorizes, obliterating all in its path to
rubble.

Maybe sky to turquoise.

Shining down on destruction.

The Rival

by Elizabeth Neal

She wore a spider broach to the party & told him it was named
"Edgar."

"Everything is 'Edgar,'" she laughed and pointed to the roses
& the guardrail over the water
& the water
& what was left of the moon

& a crunchy black spider by his head.

He loved her then; her laughter like steel & flint, her obfusca-
tions and allusions, all that she concealed
beneath her black hair & within her black tulle.

But rising above the bodice in the exquisite country between
her neck & shoulder sat a fat, rubbery mole,
the gristly bit that marred the whole.

He loathed it at once. It was selfish & confrontational. It refused
to rest behind a thigh, aside an ankle, even beneath a breast. It
longed to be regarded. It was a narcissist.

It grew as great as what was left of the Moon in his eye. It
eclipsed the satin of her cheek. It pronounced itself a rival. It
was no "Edgar."

He mourned her near perfection.

In his lust and grief he lunged and bit.

The blood, so abrupt and obscene forced itself into his mouth.
The thing itself came alive and leaping against his palette. He
caught it between the tip of his tongue and his front teeth, lest it
dance down his throat, and he spat into his palm.

She tipped him over the guardrail, her blood black in the night.
He ate the thing and grinned, teeth white and crimson as a
tiger's. He ate it before the fish stole away his victory.

<u>**Shore leave**</u>

Perhaps the sailor wouldn't be so mean

If it weren't for when he was a teen

He lost his big toe

Cause his sweat beau

Swore up and down she was clean

三滴水: **Drops of Water**

by Alice

人的一生能隐藏多少秘密呢？

泪水滴滴答答地像在轻数

大海又包容了多少人的秘密呢？

它以惊涛也拟波浪地诉说

从不停止

How many secrets can one ocean hold?

Tears break like a ticking clock.[1]

How many secrets can one life hold?

It breaks in waves [and more] waves.

It will not stop.

    -translated by Bobby

---

1 *Literal translation: tears tick tock like counting time. —though the composition of characters is really ingenious here because the symbol for didi (or 'tick') have the three drops of water radical, as of course do tears and any form of liquid.*

It's about time

by Geoff Wallace

...eyes bobbing above the waves, mouth half-open, swallowing saltwater. I was in a stilled ocean, swimming toward a city-sized wooden boat, circled by boats rowed by hundreds of men. I climbed on board and wandered into a movie theater bathroom, vintage tilework everywhere.

Rainn Wilson stood next to one urinal. "One, two, three," he said aloud, moving a finger like an abacus in his palm. "What are you doing?" I asked. "I'm counting my sperm to make sure I'm still fertile," he said. I wasn't sure if it was Rainn or Dwight Schrute. I laughed and left the bathroom.

What I found outside was less cheerful. The city-boat's streets were bronzed with rusted dust, its structures becoming more technologically complex as I neared the center of the boat--towering walkways, frozen mechanical sidewalks, and enormous glass tubes entwined like plant life choking itself.

I knew there was a park somewhere—an isolated greenbelt where people sold wares in an open-air market—but I wound up a claustrophobic stairway and entered a seemingly dead-ended room. A crowd appeared around me. "There's no way out!" a woman said, her panic feeling 1940s. "We're going to die in here!" a man yelled.

I looked around at the surprise room. Its walls were opaque glass rounded at the edges and tinted in an unusually rich shade of deep alder and smoke. Inside was what looked to be a small lab: limited furniture, a long table, machines, bookshelves.

The crowd gathered ratlike on the furniture and seemed to disappear. I remained calm and investigated the objects. There was something exceptionally unusual on the lab table—a slimy, blackened skin, rotting away; it gave off no smell. To its left was small device: a glass marble mounted on the end of a delicate mechanical arm. Further down the table were two additional machines. The larger one was boxy—like a computer—and had a small box attached to it by a cord—like a mouse. I searched for an on switch and tapped the smaller box, but nothing happened.

I turned back to the arm and studied it. A civilization of golden works spiraled down its length, as if forged by ants in thrall to a god of greater order. As I tried to comprehend the device's operation, a hologram appeared.

It was David Bowie. Not Ziggy Stardust nor the Thin White Duke nor any of his quirky incarnations—just Bowie as he appeared in his final photos. Suit and tie, hair slicked back. He lifted his right arm out at his side and flexed it slowly, like a mime, into an upward angle, as if halfway to hand waving. Reaching over with his left hand, he pointed to his right wrist. "Emit tuoba s'ti," he said, and vanished.

I thought for a moment, transfixed on the gesture. What operated with the right hand? I looked at the mouse and this time, instead of tapping it, pressed my wrist against the end closest to me, and the computer turned on.

There weren't many files on it. Opening one revealed a still image of the blackened skin. I tried using the mouse to discover additional controls, but it did nothing. As I examined the photo, I realized the point of view came from the mechanical arm's marble.

I turned to the marble and touched it, trying to see if there were some optic cables underneath, and the screen changed: a man briefly appeared then blinked out. I moved the marble again, and the screen changed again—the blackened skin twitched in the image, rising ever so slightly.

An idea struck me. I started rolling the marble. The skin continued to change, and then I knew: the marble was a camera, and the image was a time-lapse recording.

I continued rolling the marble, and the skin gradually filled, regaining color, rising into a familiar shape—it was a banana.

And there, written on its side in color-coded ink, was the key code to escape the room.

The Whale

by Eric Thralby

It was Monday we got the whale. It breathed and blinked. We pushed it, of course. But even two hundred of us couldn't budge a whale.

We did what we could. We took fishing photos, held our poles up by its mouth. I took one and sent it to the *Siuslaw News* and the *Register-Guard* both. But why publish me when we gave them Sarah Mae's three-year old? Sarah Mae dressed him up in his daddy's hat and waders. We gave him a fly fishing pole and stood him at the tip of the whale's nose. The once and future king still immortalized in driftwood and photographs in every eatery from Newport to Longbeach.

Two nights, Brady kept his eye on the whale. This was another cold November, a year after the Forgotten Year's Dreaded November, so we said, 'Brady, bundle up. You take a space heater out there with you and you sleep tight in that van.' Vanessa brought him blankets from home and told him, don't get eaten by that whale, you've got a baby to raise and he gave her belly a kiss and told her no whale was gonna stop him. She went home to her mother's. And then we got Brady drunk on the beach. The whale was a sign, he thought. He couldn't run. Here it was. All fifty feet. He looked at Vanessa's mother's house, the yellow corner just visible up the hill behind cypresses. Brady's been a player all his life. 'Be a man,' Brady, I said. He looked away from the house, then at me, then at the whale. 'I think I'm gonna,' he said.

We left him there in his van. I hiked back up the beach to my place. I waved to Brady. I waved to the whale. Do they even take us in? Certainly he saw us, but what could he possibly think?

Next morning Brady proposed to Vanessa. He got he roof of his van and shouted it through megaphone. (He's a summertime lifeguard.) It woke everyone up. But you don't leave your neighbors behind, that's what we all learned, what we all said. And if you live by the beach, you better live by the beach. We brought chairs and tables. And we set up a pastor (can't remember his name) down by the whale, not two feet from its mouth.

I couldn't see love. I watched the whale's giant eye. The film over it—fleshy and garbage-bag-like, it moved in and out of view. It had a life of its own. It swam this way over the eye, then that way. It disappeared then reappeared. Like a great black bowling ball. And we were all reflected in it, dented, almost lopsided. I touched my own eye. Were my eyes like that? We're they just as lopsided, only smaller? Will people look at my body when I die? Was it Could I die like that, wait there like that and die with people watching? It sat there, still and patient as a car park. I sat there, just as still, in a row of seats, surrounded with our town, half for a wedding and half for a whale.

Brady and Vanessa spent their first night of marital bliss staring up at a whale. They slept in Brady's van. Brady insisted he aimed to keep his word. He was a new man since the whale, the whale's turned him around. Things do that. Whales do that. He always looked afraid of the ocean, like he wasn't meant for a beach town. Now he knew where he stood.

I'd just gotten used to sleeping to whale songs. But Wednesday morning I woke up in silence. I shuffled out on my deck and saw Brady, unbalanced and pale and waving his arms. He said it shook his van. Woke him and Vanessa up. They'd never seen anything like it. Poor man was without shoes. He looked at the whale now like it a was a falling object.

A god had come down and died on our beach. Tourists poured in. Californians came in winter coats. They bought everything. We ran out of things to sell. I sold all my little lighthouses then I started selling fishing nets. Sarah Mae sold all her china, anything with whales or boats or fish. Brady sold all his bottled sloops, even ones he hadn't finished.

Money fell like stars from these people. We ate it up like shame. Who were these people? We'd spent a year in Hell. We'd all suffered the same. The depression. Misery. The madmen called it, 'The Year We Deserve. Repent!' 'Burn in Hell. Hell is here!' They flew flyers all over the streets. We stopped using the streets. They started going door to door. We all pretended we were dead.

Everything shutdown. It was the Black Plague of beach business. The Peters Brothers tarped up their go-karts and Sarah Mae burned all her seaglass.

Freaks By the Sea shutdown. Ned's Shoot 'Em shutdown. 'No

frog-legged kid? No Toad-for-Tuesdays.' Freaks was a staple. Freaks was a glue. People came down from Seattle for Freaks on the weekends. And people even from Georgia, from Kentucky, from god-knows, but people loved Freaks. We even loved Freaks. It's what turned Man around.

Courtney Man built Freaks to bring the freaks into the fold. They just came in one day, all got off the bus. A tattooed lady, an amphibian kid, a man with no bones (so he claimed), a strongman, a woman with eyes in the back of her head and a heart she held in her hands. We hated them. They walked into Mo's. The two acrobats rolled in like a wheel. They all asked for chowder. They took Mo's "captains table" all to themselves. We didn't recognize them for people. We were scared they would eat us or breed and switch out our children. But Courtney Man saw them and knew they were good. When they left, it killed Courtney. He went around breaking everyone's windshields with a bat, then he died in the snow.

Courtney drank from thirteen. He'd get drunk and forget where he was. He had a town all made up in his mind, would tell you an address that didn't exist. Find him with his eyes in the wall or flower picking and yawing his mouth. 'I live in the library.' Pull him out of the Shoot 'Em every night, dead drunk in a booth, or out in the beach grass. 'I live in the lighthouse.' Drag him out, toss him in Siuslaw. And any old girlfriend happening by would come out and yell at him—*you ne'er-do-well pantswetter shit, you vile old dog-tit licker, you snubnose horsehandling snakeinthegrass*—then we'd be there to drag him out and take him home. By morning, whether we'd showered or suited him, still he'd crawl back into the lights at the Shoot 'Em, order anything red with a little booze in it.

The freaks gave Courtney a north star. Our greatest success story, he borrowed from daddy to build Freaks and paid him back within the year. He started showing up to things on time. For the first time, he found people could depend on him. Patricia West, Sarah's sister, even took a liking to Courtney, though we warned her, though she knew, and the two went steady for a time.

The day the freaks left, the strongman had to peel Courtney off the door to the Greyhound and drag him back to us like a calf to slaughter. We piled over him and tried wave to the freaks. You could see some of them crying, the frog-legged kid and the leopard-skin lady. Courtney balled and spit like a snake. It took six of us to carry him back and throw him into the Siuslaw. I guess that's the last time Patricia ever had to yell at him. He disappeared. Three days later we found him.

We took it as it come, held our heads down and hid under tables. Kids became criminals and moms became drunks. People stopped talking to one another. No one said hello on the street. I swear some people just plain vanished. Like they wandered into the sea caves and died. We were a nowhere place. Like a mountain range had closed up around us and no one would ever hear from us again. I woke up every morning expecting the ocean'd dried up.

So we boarded up the taffy shops and burned down the driftwood. Kite sellers sold their kites back to the distributors and begged for a good price. Surf shops blacked out their windows.

Ray's ran out of food. I went three months without seeing a vegetable. I just ate canned chowder and stared at the empty sea. I took little strolls to Heceta Head, wondered, was it the impenetrable haze in the air or was it just me? I'd drive out to the dunes, or to Sea Lions' Cave, or Mo's, just to hear anybody, see anybody. Worse thing I ever saw in my life was Courtney's mom hang a dog. She tied its leash to a steak in the ground and dropped it over her fence. She watched it from her side of the fence and I watched it from across the street. You can treat it like a nightmare, mix it all up in your head, take away the hanging and put a happy dog in Courtney's arms. But what could his mom do, except hang more dogs? I've held small beings in my hands while they died. I couldn't do anything for it. It twisted around. I thought I could save it. I couldn't.

Dark days! Nothing left but to keep your head up and wait for a miracle. 'The Day the Whale Stood Still.' 'The Big Grey Blessing.' 'The Great Beached Hope.'

The police came. They wanted to help now that it died. Sure, it was a tragedy. But how much more of a tragedy if it had never come. Was it a tragedy that they crucified Christ? I sure ain't eating chowder no more.

The police asked what they could do. I said why don't we set it to sail, or give it a Viking burial? So they drove out on the beach and lined up their cruisers. The put their bumpers up against the whale, ten of them, starting out slowly, hoping to roll a whale into an ocean. And it seemed like it would. All their engine-revving, they leaned into the whale. But then they broke the skin. Their cruisers bit through its skin and then thrust into the blubber, some stuck inside and some hit bone. No crane could lift the whale. No dozer could push the whale. We got on what sides of the cruisers we could, jammed firewood under their tires, roped them to tow trucks. Maybe the cops were a little ashamed. They promised to be back with explosives. They revved up what cruisers would start and whimpered away through the trees.

School went on, though most teachers seized the opportunity of a giant whale to show off the wonders of Biology and let the kids outside to poke around its great body. Ms. Sarah Mae, cruel and scarred facially, closed the blinds. Children have to be reared. They have no nature. Nature to a child is devilish and unfiltered. If you don't bridle them, they traipse through your town breaking out windows and torturing cats. Children are shadows, otherwise wraiths—you have to light a light for them before you send them into the caves, or they'll just come out goblins again. Maybe I agree with Sarah Mae. Maybe to some, a beached whale is too much.

After school, the kids climbed the whale and slid down it. The world was their playground. Who were we to deny them? But then they sunk into the skin. 'Help, help, we're stuck in a whale!' 'Let that be a lesson, don't climb on a whale!' Some of us said let's leave them, they deserved it. But we'd encouraged them, told them live it up! But we were tired of kids. We lived in a town full of kids and never got time on our own. In the midst of all this, the kids worked it out for themselves. The big ones plucked out the little ones and they all slid down together in a string. Kids don't trust you. Tell them one minute the whale's all fun and games then run out next minute waving your hands, blowing up about bombs. Say one thing wrong and they're out to get you! They don't see the humor in it—how can you trust them? Tell you what, I'd rather see every last one of those whale-smelling kids in a lineup shaking some old lady down, or having done, than see any one of those reckless shits taking up space in the mayor's office, swearing over the Bible not to do us one dirty. I know you boys. I know your game.

Whales explode. I've heard it. The insides rot and it lifts up like an airship, then sure as chambola, boom, like hydrogen, our whole town in flames. 'I wanna be the boy who sits on the whale and explodes it!' 'I wanna be the boy who runs this town into Hell!' The fuse. 'I wanna be the boy who leads other boys far below the paths of righteousness!' 'The boy who boys remember!'

Kids that sneak in through its teeth, I'd like to see them eaten. Or hanged. I was one of those kids. What's left for you after the whale? Life after the whale. You can't be in it for long. I watched them in a spyglass. They snuck in like rats, through its gums, through its throat, to its ribs.

I was already drinking. Ned tapped on my window. He had a bag of Foster's. What could I do? Foster's, the stuff of families. And what's a little more fuel? He had Sarah Mae with him. 'Sarah Mae.' 'Eric.' She had her shirt on backwards. Ned pushed me on a Foster's. (We made it through high school together.) He typically reeked like a tire. 'What'll we do?' 'We get into that whale.' 'And then?' 'We crawl around inside it.' 'And then?' 'We never come out.' 'We're grown men. And Vanessa. And Sarah Mae. And then?' 'We become legendary.' I was drunk. And in high school you learn without peer pressure there's nothing to live for.

We snuck in on Vanessa and Brady. In the act of some new abomination. You can get away with a lot in a beach town. We took their beers out of their fridge and took them with us. Brady came out with a towel on. 'We've got to go and see the whale.' 'It's what we've all been waiting for.' 'You must come with us.'

It was dark out except the weird shine off the whale, maybe the moonlight, definitely the moonlight. We cast down into the sand and I peeled up the caution tape. I held it. It was wet. We were old. It was plastic. The gaps in its teeth were too narrow. We had to squeeze in like apes. Maybe it was easier for kids. Vanessa didn't crawl but scuttled. She looked like she'd swallowed an airbag. She had a little her inside her, clinging to her, she held a hand under her belly like she had to support it, like it could come out. She lost her hat, her shoes and her handbag, all to the teeth. We dragged her. We pushed on into the whale. I took out my flashlight and immediately saw undigested fish, drifting up and down the whale, as if through a corridor. It was an uncomfortable sound. Some maybe jiggled just on the ocean we kicked around. Or maybe the water moved on some biological process left on in the whale. It was from somewhere in the dark then, somewhere I couldn't reach my flashlight, we heard a fish jump.

Who was Sarah Mae to me? And who was she to Ned? I tote a barge all day for a living, a people barge, a 'ferry.' I watch the people get on and get off. There's too many of them. There's always too many. It's always the same people. It's the same schedule. I've seen them all come on and seen them all come off. Everyday, it's always too many people. In a way I miss the beach. I read to pass the time while they get on and get off but sometimes I'd just like to drink. It's It's the perfect life this beach life, but what are we to each other?

It was when we came to the thorax, Vanessa took a bone in the water and drew an exploding whale on the whale wall. The whale had bones, had a skeleton, but it all looked more like a cave made of flesh, like a throat full of pale stalactites, albino drippy fingers, like venomous teeth piercing down through a neck, like we were now walking into yet another mouth, one from the outside biting down on the whale. Ned boosted me and I put my hand on one of the bone-things. It felt rock-stiff but clammy. I pushed on it. There was some give, it was fragile, like maybe if you pushed it it could snap. Like a finger then some membrane would rush out.

The police would come back with their explosives and blow it all to high heaven. The famous little town with the great big explosion. If the dust ever settled, we'd sell blubber charred on hot biscuits at point of detonation. 'Come one! Come all! Chew my fat! See my legend! I could really be somebody,' said Vanessa. We pushed her and she fell in the ocean. She looked like a buoy. We forgot she was pregnant. When we helped her up she pulled us in. She hit me with a grouper.

Nights must have an end. But what if we had gotten stuck in the whale? What if we had been exploded? Did it make any difference? What didn't I have then that I do have now? I didn't want to leave the whale, but why? Why care? I loved that town but I don't think I'll go back. I left. Is it an embarrassment thing? Did I wear out my welcome? I'll never see another whale up close like that. You can write your way into something and never figure it out. It's an impossible thing, a beached whale. "Eric Thralby" means nothing to me. It's like I don't even exist. I had these friends. We got stuck in a whale together. I don't talk to those people. I don't know them anymore. Eventually, we ran out of Foster's.

We walked back toward the real mouth. A little light came in through the teeth. Sure kids could get in and out easy. But we were fat and old. No matter how hard we pushed the lips wouldn't give. I wedged my hand between two teeth. Brady and Ned pushed on me until my fingers slipped through. I felt my wrist pop out and I could squeeze the fresh air in my hand. And then hands on m hand grabbed me and pulled. And then hands like a small army of dentists slipped in through the cracks and widened the mouth so light streamed in and slipped out. 'There's more. There's more,' I said. They exploded the whale a few hours later at 3:45 p.m. It took two hundred units of dynamite. This was November 12, 1970, in Florence, Oregon.

Wikipedia:

The explosion caused large pieces of blubber to land near buildings and in parking lots some distance away from the beach. Only some of the whale was disintegrated; most of it remained on the beach for the Oregon Highway Division workers to clear away. In his report, Linnman also noted that scavenger birds, who it had been hoped would eat the remains of the carcass after the explosion, did not appear as they were possibly scared away by the noise. The explosives-expert veteran's brand-new automobile, ironically purchased during a "Get a Whale of a Deal" promotion in a nearby city, was flattened by a chunk of falling blubber.[2]

I asked the mayor of Portland, at that time Terry Schrunk, would he be sending the people by droves or in swarms? By bus load or truckload? He said he'd come himself. I have pictures now of me and the whale and me and the mayor.

What I loved most was the heat I felt in him. When he looked into my eyes, I told him, Look, I'm sorry, I'm not strong enough. He knew we couldn't help him. He just had to die there. And then we blew him up.

<u>Gangrene</u>

It's a bit of a misnomer

This disease affecting sea-roamers

Your skin'll turn black

From a traumatic attack

Not quite as poetic as Homer

Who can know for how long you've been falling

by Maya McOmie

Who can know for how long you've been falling—

until the vastness, dim and spare,

discretely legible and worn with use,

is no longer referred to by its real name.

You were drawn in, lungs first. Of course you sank.

Perceptibly finite, repurposed, just

like everything else. But all those who sink

were at first needed. Not your fault if the

blood is too warm, and love too circular

to last you. If only there had been less

of it all. Some day, you keep thinking,

you too will arrive at its deep deep core.

Wastewater

by Geoff Wallace

"What's Wastewater?" I asked. We were in the New Student Dome. Your hair was a rectilinear waterfall, drowning the crowd's noise. I was an RA.

"Wastewater is a program," you said, gesturing to a laptop with no screen. "It replaces your memories. But not all at once."

You paused to look at the murals along the dome: rain and wings more dinosaur than bird.

"And some memories come back, only to be replaced again."

I gave you a room key and you left, jet black hair frozen in place. I turned to the other new students—they were talking about RPGs and doing coke, but all the new coke did was make them instantly fatter. Their eyes glazed, they nearly forgot their new home was underwater, built among the wreckage of lost ships and older domes.

Walking helical ramps through the dorm hives, I found Snoop Dogg's room. His smile was almost as warm as his red-yarn halter top. I looked over his poems—he was in love with the word fastidious. One poem was about sprinting.

"You were so fast!" I exclaimed. He smiled like a woman or a cat.

Later his friends came over and we watched videos of Snoop's greatest knife fights.

"You were so fast!" I exclaimed. Snoop laughed. "Oh no," I said, putting my hand over my face like a cartoon robot, "I'm repeating myself!" We laughed.

A friend handed me Snoop's championship double butterfly knife. I opened the rusted blades and they snapped back over my finger. The room recoiled, the men bellowing.

"Don't worry," I said. "I've done this before. See?" I lifted the blades off my skin, revealing a white scar. I traced its path, but I couldn't remember anything about the war.

On the street outside, I looked around—the dorms were all part of the dome's hospital. Someone had rebuilt Machu Picchu a few blocks away, decay and all. As cars sped past, I realized I was pissing all over the sidewalk and walked back inside the dorms. The bathroom had too many toilets, its tiles a green as mute as libraries; the bathroom kept going, its corridors winding away.

It's toilets everywhere, I thought, but they're all so clean. I walked to the new urinals that were flatscreen TVs. How does this work? I wondered. Do I piss on it to turn it on?

Men did business or drugs a few stalls over. A man who was dead to me entered the bathroom and approached an exposed toilet. He knelt down, examining the porcelain. That guy, I thought. He's totally…that guy. I ignored him, focusing on the TV and some show with comedians doing stand-up among tombs.

A black cat wandered past the stalls. I flushed and searched for the sinks. The man had built a pyramid mound of tissue paper around the toilet, leaving the bowl's opening as the mound's plateau. The cat monitored the trash, ensuring each person's waste made it in before they left.

I went to my mom's penthouse overlooking the city, the apartment building a giant white sword jammed into an old ship. People celebrated inside. "Your brother's going to need a new job!" my mom cheered.

I sipped champagne as we gazed at the sea clouds below. "I thought they just hired him?"

Something sinuous beyond the glass caught my eye. As I turned toward it, I remembered what you'd told me: *Wastewater is a program. It replaces your internal organs with chocolate and roses.* Suddenly, a waterspout descended on the city, wrecking roofs and antique ships.

"This couldn't happen in my home town," I said, nonchalant. "Not in Everett. But wasn't this Everett?"

"What do you mean?" my aunt asked, drunk.

My phone rang three times: a number from Everett. I didn't answer it. The waterspout split apart and slipped out of the dome, moving deeper into the ocean. As the dome's skin began to close over the wounds, I saw the ocean beyond—it was full of waterspouts. "This home isn't home," I said, feeling the champagne bubbles rise and dissipate beneath my chin. "But I think that I'm home."

I finished my glass as I gazed up at the dome, the cracks smoothing into a new sky like a clean white scar.

Kissed by the Sea

by Z.B. Wagman

Long ago, in a secluded village by the sea, there lived a boy. Every morning the boy would wake up before dawn and cook breakfast for his parents. He would gather his father's fishing gear and help his dad into his great seal-skin coat. Just as the sun began to rise, the boy would stand in the doorway and wave as his father trudged down the hill to the nearby port. For as long as he could the boy would stand there, wishing he could join his father on the ocean. But soon enough his mother would call him and the boy would have to return to his chores.

The boy's day was busy: he fed the goats, weeded the garden, cleaned house, and made repairs to his father's gear. His mother worked next to him, joking and laughing through the day's tasks. But he was always distracted. His mind was focused on the small sailboat in which his father was sailing. As the sun began to set, the boy watched for his father, stooped under the day's catch, as he made his way back up the hill. The boy would help clean and cook the fish as his father told him of the day on the water.

On the boy's thirteenth birthday he woke up early like every other morning, only to find his parents already awake. They had made a special breakfast for him: eggs and ham fresh from the market—not a fish in sight. He wolfed it hungrily, hardly noticing the stony silence of his parents across the table. Finally his father spoke. "Son," he said in his deep rumble. "I think it's time you joined me on the water."

The boy couldn't believe his ears, his dreams had finally come true. "Yes!" hHe shouted, launching himself to his feet.

"Settle down," his father laughed. "I got ya' something that might help." He pulled a brown package out from under the table.

The boy tore back the wrapping. It was a seal-skin coat of his very own. The oily fur felt soft beneath his fingers. It was perfect.

As his mother helped him don his new coat, she knelt down before him and caught his eye. "Promise me you'll come back."

"Mom," the boy laughed. "Nothing's going to happen."

And minutes later the boy and his father were headed down the hill towards the village. If he had turned around, the boy might have caught sight of his mother standing in the doorway, a glimmer of tears on her cheeks.

#

The sailboat seemed like a palace to the boy. Its single mast stretched upwards like a tower and its white sail blazed like a beacon across the blue sky. It promised adventure with every flap of the wind.

After they boarded the boat, his father showed the boy his job for the day: he was to be in charge of the rigging. The boy's heart leapt with pride. It was an important job, it meant that he would be controlling the sail. And he swore that he would do it better than any job he had ever done.

Then they were off. Sailing out through the jaws of the bay, the boy could feel the ocean come alive beneath him. Every swell seemed magical to him. As the boat swung out into open water, two porpoises swam up alongside them, jumping and spinning through the air. The boy let out a giddy laugh.

"It's said that they were chosen by the ocean. They bring good luck to any fisherman who sees them," his father said with a smile of his own. "It's especially lucky to spot them on your first voyage." The boy stared in awe as the creatures gave a final leap and vanished beneath the waves.

As the morning passed, the boy proved himself to be a good sailor and a good fisherman. Within minutes of casting his line the boy had caught his very first fish. It was a huge rockfish, bigger than any his father had brought home. And though the man grumbled about "beginner's luck," the boy could tell that his father was pleased. By noon, they had caught more fish than ever before and the father was in a celebratory mood. He took the boy behind the wheel and soon had the boy running the boat at full steam. He was a natural sailor and the father complimented himself on having a son who had inherited so much of his talent.

When the two broke for lunch both were in high spirits. The boy had spent so many days dreaming about sailing but he never could have imagined the thrill that came with it. While he was out on the water, whether behind the wheel or just casting his line, the boy felt a sense of belonging. Never before had anything come so naturally to him. He wished he could stay out there forever.

As the two polished off their smoked fish, a loud a cacophony erupted from the village. The church bells peeled out over the water in a warning that every sailor knew: storm brewing. As the boy stared back towards the noise, he felt a small flutter of fear. He was not sure if he was ready to face the fury of a storm. And it seemed as if he wasn't the only one: as he watched, the other boats from their fleet began to turn back for the safety of the bay.

But the storm seemed to have other ideas. Before the boats had turned about, storm clouds rumbled over head. They moved faster than any clouds the boy had seen, dark and angry—more like chariots brimming with lightning.

"Son!" His father's booming voice pulled the boy away from the plight of the other boats. He was needed in their own fight for survival.

The wind cracked at their sails. He could barely hear his father's orders over the roar of the storm, commanding him from line to line across the deck. Lightning flickered in the sky above them and the boy could feel the swells beneath them getting deeper and deeper, as if the ocean wanted to swallow them whole.

Suddenly, a blast of wind ripped the line from his hand. The mast above him splintered and the boat tilted into the waves. The boy screamed. He knew this was it. He closed his eyes and let all of his terror come pouring out into the storm…and the world froze.

Lightning hung in mid-air as the boat teetered towards its watery doom. Silence broke over everything. Only the boy seemed immune. He gazed around, taking in the broken mast and the frozen waves. Even his father stood frozen: hands on the wheel, eyes bulging in fear. And then something else moved.

At the back of the boat, standing on top of the waves, was a woman. Ethereal in her beauty, she radiated a blueish light. Slowly she strode towards the boy, each step casting small ripples across the frozen waves.

The boy felt compelled towards her, his legs moving on their own accord. He stopped at the edge of the boat, barely able to stand under the weight of her gaze. Her eyes were the deepest of greens, with something dark swimming in their core. He knelt as she stepped onto the deck and the whole boat groaned underneath them. In a motion that could have lasted eons, the woman leaned forward and placed her lips on the boy's forehead.

His head exploded in pain, radiating outward from that kiss. The boy reeled as darkness overwhelmed him. The woman vanished.

The boy recovered to find himself flat on the deck of their boat. Above him, the mast reached up into the blue sky. The storm was gone. Their boat undamaged. As he got to his feet, he saw bobbing in the water around them the other boats of their fleet. It was as if there hadn't been a gust of wind all day.

The boy's father stood at the helm of the boat, exactly where he had been during the storm. For a second the boy thought him still frozen until the man's eyes flashed over him. "It's time to go home," he said. But the command had lost some of its power.

"Why?" The boy objected, it seemed as if the danger was passed. Why couldn't they reclaim the fun they had been having before the storm? But his father didn't answer him. Instead he just swung the boat back towards land.

As soon as the boat pulled into port, the boy flung their catch over his shoulder and made to climb the steep hill home. After a good day fishing, the port was usually alive with the calls of merchants and sailors. Today however there was only silence. As the boy looked around, he noticed all of the villagers staring back at him. They recoiled away from his gaze, unable to meet his eye. The boy hoisted his bag and began his climb.

#

From then on, the boy was an outcast in the village. Whenever he appeared, the rest of the village cowered away from him. But this did not stop the him: he began every morning with the long walk down the hill. In the beginning he was joined by his father, but more and more he found himself walking alone. Every morning, as he swung his boat into the ocean, he was greeted by a pair porpoises. And every night he always returned with the biggest catch, no matter how many other sailors went out that day.

"Tell me: how was the ocean today?" It was the question that his mother always asked him when he returned to the house on the hill.

"It had its ups and downs," was his ritual reply. And then he would tell her everything about his day on the water. By the end of his story, his mother would always be in tears.

His father had a different response to his son's newfound life on the ocean. Before the boy's daily story had even begun, the man would already be deep in his cups. He avoided eye contact with his son and even went so far as to curse his son's skill on the water. Most nights ended with him stumbling blindly to bed or worse, passing out in his chair at the table.

"What's wrong with Dad?" The boy asked his mother after one particularly bad evening.

"People fear what they don't understand."

The boy began staying out later and later, too depressed to come home. Between his mother's crying and his father's cursing, the boat became a much more friendly place. It's gentle rocking lulled him to sleep as the keening of the whales wove into his dreams.

He fished less and less, more content to swim amongst the fish than to pull them above water. The porpoises became his playmates, always ready to gambol about whenever the boy dove beneath the waves. And in the evenings, after the day's adventures, he would sit and watch the jellyfish light up the ocean, their eerie glow almost ghost-like beneath the waves. This was home now. This was where he belonged.

\#

Time passed quickly for the boy. He did not know when the anniversary of the big storm came—he was too busy frolicking with the porpoises. They darted through the water just out of his reach. It was a game they played often: if ever he caught one, it dove deep as the boy struggled to cling to its back. Only when he finally let go, or was on the verge of losing consciousness, would the porpoise turn back towards the surface.

On one of these dashes skyward, the boy caught sight of a dark shadow above them. A dinghy, much smaller than the boat that he had borrowed from his father, was making its way towards his craft. The villagers had long since gone out of their way to avoid him. Never had any of them dared come near his boat.

The boy gasped as his head broke above water mere feet from the foreign vessel. As air rushed back into his lungs, he heard the stranger onboard give a shout of surprise. The boy turned in the water, keen on seeing who dared disturbed him. To his surprise he recognized the haggard face that stared back at him from the oars.

"Dad?"

The man didn't respond. He just slid the oars into their locks and stared at his son.

"What're you doing here? Do you need more fish?"

"No," the man finally spoke, his voice more gravelly than the boy remembered. "Your mother asked me to come."

"Mom asked…" The boy trailed off. Confusion washed over him. What could his mother possibly want from him? Wanting more answers, he pulled himself over the side of the boat.

"You're to come home now. No more fishing or sailing," his father said as he watched the boy settle onto the bench across from him. "Not now, not ever. She said she'd explain everything. Said it was important…" The man trailed off, his fingers fiddling with the oar shafts.

"Never sail?" The boy didn't understand. "But why?"

The man shook his head, "Dunno. Said she'd tell you when you got home"

The boy looked around him. He could just see the shadow of one of his porpoise friends deep beneath them. "No. No way." He moved to dive back in the water but his dad grabbed his hand.

"She begged me. Begged me to come get you." A breeze licked at the man's scraggly gray hair. In that instant the boy saw not his father, but a tired old man.

"I-I'll come by next week. I'll bring some fish. But I've got to go now. Tell mom…Tell her something from me." He moved again to leave but his dad did not let go. In the distance, a bell started clanging.

"Please son, it's important," the old man rasped.

But it was too late. Other bells took up the cry as storm clouds began to gather. It was all too familiar to the boy. He spun to face his father. "What's happening?"

But the man was already panicking. He reached for the oars, finally letting go of his son, and struggled with the locks. "We need to go."

The boy had had enough. He launched himself over to his own boat as lightning crackled through the sky. He landed hard on the deck as the boat began to buck under the waves. Another fork of lightning lanced across the sky, this one pummeling straight into his mast. The timber creaked under the impact and in an instant fire sprung up everywhere.

As the flames rushed across the deck, the boy did all he could to quell them. He pulled the burning sails from the rigging, casting them overboard. He tossed water on the spreading flames but, even as the fire sizzled, he knew that the he was in trouble.

He took to the helm, driving the boat into the deepening swells of the ocean. The giant waves washed overboard ripping away anything that wasn't tied down. Still the flames spread and, even worse, the ocean rocked so hard the the boy lost his grip on the wheel. As the boat jerked away from him, teetering over the edge of the deepest swell yet, the boy screamed.

And for the second time, the boy found himself in a frozen landscape.

A giant wall of water loomed before him and he knew that if the spell lifted his boat would be cast asunder.

From the middle of this giant waves pulsed an eerie blue light. As if from an egg, the wave cracked open and the woman emerged. There was little thought of her beauty now. A fish would not linger on the beauty of a shark. As she smiled down at the boat before her, the boy shivered.

"What do you want from me?" His voice rang small across the frozen landscape.

Her voice hammered back at him. "Nothing but a choice."

"A choice?"

"You have been shown the beauty of the ocean. And the anger. And I have seen both beauty and anger in you. Which will you choose?"

"I don't understand."

The woman smiled again, "You must choose where to spend your days. You can come with me to the bottom of the ocean and live a joyous life amongst the whales and porpoises. Or you can return to land, frightened and confused, never to sail again."

The boy looked again at the towering wall of water before him. "If I chose the land you'll let me go? You won't drag me under with the storm?"

"You will be safely returned to harbor."

"Or I can live under the water. With you."

"With me and with the others who have chosen the sea."

It was a tempting decision. In many ways it was one he had already made. He already lived on the ocean. And everyone in the village already feared him. Who would even notice that he was gone?

"What about my dad?"

The woman's smile wavered. She cast her eyes out over the ocean where a single frozen wave began to move. On its crest, the boy could just make out the shape of a tiny dinghy. "He *could* be saved. But the ocean must claim someone today."

\#

When the storm broke, the boy's mother found her husband washed up on shore. He was waterlogged and half-drowned but he was alive. She helped him to his feet and they embraced. There were no need for words.

As her husband turned to make the long journey up the hill, she paused a moment to sit on the end of the dock, her feet dangling in the water. Occasionally it would seem to pull at her, as if trying to sweep her off her perch. She watched the waves roll in; they were so small that it was as if there had never been a storm at all.

A chirping sound from the water in front of her broke her trance. She turned to see a porpoise leap into the air and performed a single magnificent backflip. The woman smiled as the beast slipped back beneath the waves.

"Goodbye," she whispered as she climbed to her feet. "I hope your choice brings you as much happiness as mine did." She turned started the long walk up the hill, there were goats to feed and a husband to care for. She was headed home.

Sisters Sleek and Sharp

by Leanna Moxley

On late summer afternoons, when the water gets real still the mermaids surface, the spines on their backs rising out of the lake. My brother says he's gonna catch one, even prowls the shore with a hook he's fashioned out of an old broom handle and some coat hangers. He hauls a plastic trash can with him to keep a mermaid in once he's caught it. What he plans to do with her after that, I have no idea. Anyway, it doesn't matter, cuz they'll never let him near them. They don't show their lovely faces to him, only their fearsome backs. Why would they? He's loud and impatient and likely to hit anything that startles him, and his imagination is sorely limited.

I wait till he gets bored and goes inside and then I wade along the shore, pulling up long green lake grass to braid into a crown. It's quiet, air heavy over the lake. I hear a splash behind me and turn, nearly slipping in the mud, and there are two of them, smiling at me with glinting eyes and needle-pointed teeth. One has dark hair tangled through with weeds and algae. The other is bald as a fish, skin the same golden green as the bass my brother leaves gasping in a bucket after he tears them off his fishing hooks. Seems like this would make her ugly, but the scales suit her, all shimmery in the sunlight. She wraps her arms around her tangle-haired sister and they bob there for a minute, watching me, before they flip their tails up and slip below the surface.

If my brother means to catch one he'll have to deal with those fins, sharp enough to cut a grown man's rough hands. With the spikes on their backs and all their many teeth they're fearsome, it's true, but I'm not afraid. I sit so still in the water to watch them, not minding the minnows that nibble at the freckles on my knees.

The mermaids are never alone. I've seen as many as five at once, jumping and racing each other across the lake. I wonder what it's like to have so many sisters. I try swimming like they do, flipping my legs up, going for a leap, landing with a flop. By the far shore a few heads surface and their laughter echoes over to me, high and skittery. I crawl outta the water and flop on the grass. Red and gold flash behind my lids as the sun dries me and the shame of my clumsiness melts in a drowsy haze.

Later, I steal one of Mama's leg warmers out of her dresser and pull it over both my legs. I practice hopping down the carpeted hall in my new tail of burgundy wool.

"Stop flopping around like a dirty animal and walk on the two legs god gave you," Mama says when she catches me.

The next day I sneak down to the lake with my wool tail anyway, but it goes loose in the water and tangles up my legs. I pull it off me and practice holding my breath instead, diving deep with my eyes wide open. Mama would yell if she knew I was doing it, tells me the dirt and germs will make me blind. But what are eyes for if not for looking, and I've never seen anything as gorgeous as the light coming down from the surface, how it shines through flecks of mud and algae and turns everything around me to sparkling gold.

At the surface the water is warm, but slip down only a few feet and the chill creeps in, colder the closer I move to the center, to the heart of the deep. I map the bottom with my hands and toes and water-stung eyes. If I go down far enough I'll find the place where the mermaids live. But my body won't cooperate, my limbs betraying and scrambling me back up to the surface.

A mercrowd gathers nearby. I hear them giggling. Swirls of cold water brush my sides as their tails swish past me. I try again and again, coming up to gasp for air before I flip back down and kick toward the bottom. I can feel how close they are around me, closer than they've ever come before. Slick fingers touch my arms, my hips, my toes. Their knotted hair clouds my vision. I can't tell how many there are. I burst to the surface to gasp for another breath. The mermaids circle and I look around at them, blinking water out of my eyes. Their faces look so human that, like a fool, I imagine they might start speaking.

When I dive this time small hands grip me. I open my eyes in the murky water. There are mermaids grabbing onto my arms. They smile their toothy smiles and tug me down. They've seen how hard I'm trying, and now they wanna help. Mermaids hold my legs and sides, the swish swish swish of their tails troubles the water. A bubble of panic rises in my throat and I try to pull my arms away, but their grip is fierce. We're deeper than I've ever made it -- the light doesn't filter this far down, the cold grips me, my lungs strain. I open my mouth to scream and water pours in but, strangely, doesn't choke me -- flows in and out like air. And there is a light now -- it's coming from below. We are headed toward it, headed home.

Something small and hard pings off the back of my head. Without warning the hands are gone and I am suspended in a flurry of writhing fins that slice and sting as they graze my skin. Somehow my face bursts to the surface. I cough up water and suck down air. More sharp little pings catch me on the shoulder and cheek.

I jerk my head around and see my brother on the shore. He tosses another fistful of gravel and the mermaids move around me in a disoriented swirl.

"Get!" he yells, his voice carrying clear across the water. "Get on out of here you little demons!"

"Stop it!" I yell back at him.

Most of the mermaids are gone now, but the two that first smiled at me still bob in front of me, beckoning with their hands, glinting and gleaming all lovely in the sunlight. They swim closer and put their cool fingers on my face, making little chirps and titters in my ears. I wanna know what they're thinking and I wanna see what they could show me and I wanna go with them but I can already feel the sinking in my stomach. It's their faces, how they look so human - it tricks you into thinking they're something they're not.

When the rock catches her right in the side of her shining bald head her eyes go dull in an instant. Her sister screams, lunging toward the shore, and my brother scrambles up the bank and runs for the house. I reach for the floating body, gather her in the crook of my arm, and swim for the bank. But when I haul her out and lay her on the ground it's clear she's already dead.

Mama's come out of the house, roused by all the commotion. She walks down the hill and kneels next to me, shading her eyes with one hand. My brother trails behind her with his head down, kicking at the dirt, avoiding the glares I'm sending his way.

"What a beautiful creature," she says, touching the tip of the mermaid's nose. She cuts her eyes towards my brother, "what a shame."

He snorts defiantly. "They were trying to drown her!"

"They weren't," I say, "they just wanted to show me something." I look around for the other one, thinking maybe she'll be nearby, crying for her sister. But the lake has gone still as glass again. The breeze on my damp skin makes me shiver.

Mama clucks her tongue. "It's impossible to tell with wild things, but at least you're safe." She gets to her feet and picks up the mermaid by the neck, dangling the body at arms length. The head rolls loose, fin dripping slime, eyes as empty as the high blue sky. "No use wasting good meat," she says, "I'll make us a stew for dinner."

<u>**Scurvy**</u>

I'm losing my teeth, molars then canines

Awful's the sight, futile's the dine

My smile got many gaps

Could you perhaps

Spare some fruit, just one lime?

Washout

by Mike Santiago

As a grizzled and broad shouldered captain sat at the plank of his own sinking ship, he muttered to himself, "I am no longer needed in this world, for now I must acquiesce my fate."

Without notice, a second round of whistles pierced the air. And suddenly, a volley of cannon fire collided with the hull of that very same ship. It rocked back and forth as absolute decimation was the only outcome. The now battered ship began to quickly take in water. The captain stood up from the plank and walked towards the bow. With his head held low, he saw the corpses of the men who first embarked on this suicide mission littering the deck and making every step an obstacle.

Arriving at the bow, he focused his attention to the horizon as he reached down towards his holster. He pulled out his flintlock and placed it firmly against his temple. And for a few brief seconds, he hesitated.

"Words can not acquit me from my men, my country, or my family. My very darkness not only consumed me, but everyone and everything I've touched thus far. May everyone's mind now remain at ease that this scourge is now over," he stated with a solemn stare.

Squeezing the trigger slowly, he released not only the cast iron bullet, but his ravaged mind as well. His body plummeted to the ground as the now lifeless ship descended into the watery abyss below. For now, Davy Jones Locker would be the final resting place of the man who sold the world.

However, the captain's fate was sealed only weeks prior to this disastrous skirmish that left little vestige behind.

"Elizabeth... Elizabeth... Damn it woman, WHERE ARE YOU!?"

As Captain Avery raced feverishly through every vestibule of the dilapidated barrack, he could hear the passionate moans coming from a dimly lit room at the end. He ran towards the space and kicked in the door to find his wife, Elizabeth, copulating with one of the king's lord commanders. Without hesitation, Avery unsheathed a hidden dagger and planted it into the back of the lord commander. Over and over again, the dagger found itself piercing the now lifeless corpse with Avery's wife screaming underneath. His calloused and wavering grip released the dagger, and as it fell to floor, he began to scream. The blood on his face washed away as tears began to shed. For not only did he find his wife in bed with another man, but he swiftly came to the realization that he would now be labeled an enemy to the throne he once swore allegiance to.

"Elizabeth, do you not realize what you've done? What I've done? I have brought about the demise of our very lives through your treacherous acts!"

The faint voices of the admirals guards drew closer as their foot steps rattled the dank halls of the barracks. With each thud drawing closer to that very room, Avery told his wife to hide inside of a nearby chest.

The guards burst into the room and saw the dagger clenched in his hands as blood dripped from the tip. As the guards began to unsheathe their swords, Avery whipped out a pair of flintlock pistols and dropped the guards in their place. Without a second thought, he called for Elizabeth, grabbed her hand and ran through the dank corridors.

Outside the barracks, Avery's steed awaited as he mounted the stallion and pulled his wife atop the rear of it. They set off to their residence to fetch their two young children, Ezra and Noah. As they drew closer to their manor, Avery began to formulate a plan that could grant his family safe passage. He planned to retrieve every loyalist he had left to help him and his family set sail to the Nassau, better known as the paradise for pirates, but he anticipated that the king's fleet would soon pursue an unprecedented manhunt for them.

"Ezra... Noah... boys... come to father and make haste!"

Tugging at the reigns of his horse, he came to a full stop to see his two boys hanging by a noose on the porch of their estate, which was now engulfed in flames. He screamed with agony as his only two children swayed back and forth from a supporting beam. Ezra, their first born, had a dagger plunged into his heart with a letter on the other end of it.

Avery stumbled and staggered as he made his way to their now lifeless bodies. Pulling out his moist dagger, he cut down both of his boys and laid them side by side. He then removed the dagger that was planted firmly into Ezra's chest and began to read the letter.

"By order of the King,

Captain Avery and his family shall be laid to rest for his crimes against the throne. All assets are to be seized immediately.

Every loyalist found aiding the fugitive will find their fate sealed and executed."

The letter boiled his blood and rattled his bones as he crumpled it up and tossed it into one of the nearby flames that now consumed the home that he had created for him and his family. Elizabeth ran over to Avery to provide solace, but his temper was brewing and with every ounce of energy he could muster – he raised his arm and pulled the trigger. She collapsed as an expertly placed shot found its way into her abdomen.

"AVERY, how... how could you?" Elizabeth muttered.

"Woman, you have taken everything away from this family. As I return from a skirmish, I find you... you whore... fornicating with another man. Now look! Our two boys have suffered dearly, and everything I've worked so hard for has been wasted away by your inability to stay faithful. You bloody wretch! You tore our life asunder," Avery proclaimed as his wife was bleeding out only a few meters away.

He stood up, adjusted his posture, and made his way over to a nearby shed to fetch a spade so that he could put his children to rest.

"Avery, I wish I could retract my actions, for I love you dearly. If I knew what travesty would occur, I would have forgone my heinous actions. I thought you were lost at sea my beloved. The lord commander had said as much, and that your ship was now nestled in the depths of Davy Jones Locker. You see, my love,

I thought you had perished," Elizabeth explained as her last breathe was drawing near.

The stark realization began to settle in that maybe Avery had taken extreme measures without resolve through proper discourse. Clenching the spade in his right hand, he looked back at his wife as a tear trickled down his cheek. He now knew that he alone was responsible for his family's demise, but he also knew that now there was no turning back, for his fate was sealed. His only responsibility in that moment was to put his family to rest in front of his home set ablaze.

He began pounding the spade against the earth and dug with all his might; chucking the dirt to his side. For nearly an hour, he worked his way digging three plots. First was Ezra, his oldest and wisest child, was laid in the first plot. Then it was Noah, and lastly his wife Elizabeth in the third.

"God, why have you forsaken me to lose my children, for they were too young to depart this blasphemous world so soon. And my wife, why couldn't I have used rationale versus barbaric instinct. What do I do now? All I have left are my men. But only if they choose to remain loyal to me and not the throne. But should I reveal the truth to them? For I am now a fugitive with no will to move forward. Grant me the strength my lord," he said hopelessly as his hands began to tremble frantically.

Mounting his steed, he rode off to a nearby encampment, which was hopefully where many of his crewmen could be found. However, he was unsure who would swear allegiance to his plight now that he's been marked an enemy by the king. Regardless, he knew he had no other options left.

After a five hour journey south of his estate, he came to the camp and shouted out for his men. "Boys, your captain has returned. Come now, I must ask you something of the utmost urgency. BOYS!" Avery shouted with a baffled look on his face. His gaze fixated in every direction, yet not a single soul was in sight. Walking through the camp ever so cautiously, he heard the loud wisp of incoming cannon fire from a docked vessel nearby. Narrowly dodging the blast radius, he made haste back to his horse and rode off. Not knowing where he was going to go next or where his crewmen were, he decided - as a last ditch effort - to visit the local tavern to search for his men.

Avery's crew wasn't comprised of the most noble and up-standing men the fleet had to offer, however, they were fiercely loyal and absolute experts at seafaring. Drawing close to the tavern, he dismounted and ran inside to find many of his men pissed drunk.

As he barged through the door, he shouted, "Boys, I need you all to come with me as we have now been marked enemies by the king, and he requires our very lives now to satiate his lust for revenge."

"Captain, we've just returned not only a fortnight ago. What are our crimes? We've not committed any treachery against the throne," a bewildered and drunk crew member said.

'The details shall come later, for now we must set sail to Nassau. Will you all stand with me one last time? Where is the Euphrates?" he confidently stated.

"Aye Captain, we shall face this scourge together and make way to that dastardly island! The Euphrates is docked nearby in Gold Bay" another crew member said sternly.

In the dark recesses of Avery's mind, he knew he had convoluted the truth and manipulated his own crew to abed him in his escape, but he knew that the time would soon come where he would have to reveal the exact details of what had transpired. He just hoped that he could set sail without any interference. After all, the king already seemed to be ten paces ahead at every turn as the encampment was now under siege, too.

Now, Avery was 135 men strong, and determined to alter the trajectory of his shattered destiny. They mounted their horses and rode off to Gold Bay to retrieve they're esteemed vessel, the Euphrates. Although retrieving the Euphrates may not prove to be an easy mission, it was the only course they could now take.

As they arrived at Gold Bay, which was only a few kilometers south of the tavern, Avery was in a state of shock that the king had yet to send a battalion to the bay. Despite being in a perpetual state of suspense and expecting an ambush that did not come, he screamed with all his might, "Men, leave the horses behind and board the Euphrates. We must set sail immediately, and embark to Nassau."

His men dismounted and began running to the vessel to prepare it for voyage. With in a relatively short space of time, the sails were released, freely billowing in the wind. Next, the anchor was withdrawn from the sea floor and the cannon doors were opened. With Avery at the helm of the Euphrates, he was now confident that the crew could set sail, but he was unaware of what was awaiting just beyond the horizon.

At the kings behest, a fleet of thirty ships awaited 150 clicks away from Avery's position. The fleets sole intent was to reduce the Euphrates to a catatonic state. The unwavering captain was absolutely unaware of their fate and what was awaiting them in the distance.

The Euphrates was now at the mercy of not only the unrelenting waves of the sea, but to the insurmountable feat that now faced them. And with a howling crack, a cannon hit the hull of the Euphrates. It rocked the ship from port to starboard without any remorse. Water gushed in and began to fill the bowls of the ship.

Avery realized that his defeat was imminent as his ship was now taking on water. He made his way to the plank of his now sinking vessel, and he contemplated the very choices that disintegrated his very life in a flash. His mind raced with somber thoughts of his wife and children. Nassau would not come, for it was time to accept what he now had left and that he had become a complete washout.

"I am no longer needed in this world, for now I must acquiesce my fate," he muttered.

The Selkie

by Azalea Micketti

Once upon a time...

There was a small village at the farthest edge of the smallest island on the outskirts of a small archipelago in the northern most point of the North Sea.

The earth of this island was rocky and barren, and there was little that grew there. There were even fewer animals that made it their home. But there was one that thrived.

The selkie.

Now to us the selkie looks just like another seal, sleek and grey with it's fine whiskers and sad eyes. But selkies are different, because once a month they shed their skin and take a human shape. The selkie is powerful and strong in the water, and just as beautiful and fierce when they are human. It is said that at one time selkies were just seals who were so powerful curious about life on land they learned how to shed their skin so they could walk amongst us. But others say that they used to be human, and some powerful magic was cast on them by the Finfolk to turn them into seals.

Selkies and seals have always lived in harmony upon the rocky shores, and within the seas. It used to be that selkies visited humans as well. We had festivals every full moon, the day the selkies shed their skin. And all that day and into the night the selkies would make their way upon the land and into the village. There was singing and dancing and feasting all night long, and come morning the selkies would slip out of the village, back into their skin and off into the sea.

But one year a terrible trick was played on a member of the selkie clan, and it all went sour.

One of the boys who used to live in this village went by the name of Malcolm. Malcolm MacCodrum was, in looks, one for the ballads. His skin was fair and his eyes were pale, and he had bright ginger hair. But in his heart he had a darkness that twisted his thoughts and made him cruel. Because he was beautiful, and because he was confident, Malcolm had many friends. Perhaps friends is the wrong word. He had followers. There were other boys—not so handsome, and not so confident—who held onto his coattails and and followed in his wake.

One month, as the moon festival was being prepared, Malcolm took it upon himself to wait at the waters edge and spy on the selkies as they emerged from the sea. This was something that had never been done, for selkies are magical first and foremost, and it was said a curse was laid on he who espied the change without permission. But Malcolm was cruel and he did not listen to those who warned him. So he waited, and he watched, and for the first time in human memory a sacred transformation was witnessed by one on the outside.

What Malcolm learned was this: the transformation of selkie to human is not like that of the wolf-man from Brittany. It is more like a snake shedding it's skin. For that is what the selkie do, they shed their skin and in doing so take on a human form. It is not right to say that they become human, because no matter what you look like your essence remains the same.

Malcolm watched as a particularly large and elegant seal began to shed it's skin. The form it took on was that of a tall dark woman. Her hair was long and thick and a shocking silvery grey in color, the same as was the skin at her feet. Despite the color of her hair, she was not aged but appeared as a woman in her prime. She lifted the skin she had shed, folded it carefully, and tucked it into a space between two rocks. From the same spot she retrieved a long gown in a simply green wool, which she pulled over her head before climbing up the shore towards the village. She wore no shoes.

Malcolm watched her go, making sure she was out of sight before he clambered back the way she had come. He reached into the space and retrieved the seal skin from where it lay comfortably cradled amongst the stones. The grey of the skin matched almost perfectly the grey of the rocks. Malcolm, thinking only of himself, took the pelt and tucked it into the front of his shirt. It was cold and slick against his skin. Not knowing how many other selkies might emerge that morning, he took his prize and ran back to the village.

Malcolm told no one he had taken the skin, except those

other boys he knew were too afraid of him to speak a word. The boys passed the skin amongst themselves, feeling it's fine texture and desecrating it's softness with the oil from their fingers. Finally one of the other boys asked Malcolm what he planned to do with it.

"I will hide it," he said. "And when the moon has risen and the festival is over she will not be able to return to the sea."

And indeed the festival took place. There was feasting and dancing and merriment between human and selkie alike. And when it came time for them to return to their watery home, the selkies left the village in twos and threes, tired and content.

Rona, for that was the selkie's name, searched for her skin all night long, but when the next pale grey dawn crept with withered fingers over the horizon she was still looking. She knew no selkie would touch another's skin, but neither did she want to believe that a human would be so cruel. She keened for the loss of skin and innocence alike.

When the sound of her keening reached the waking villagers they shivered in their cottages. The sun rose with a quiet desperation upon a world that was a little bit darker than it had been before.

Now, Malcolm had a twin sister who was as fair and beautiful as he was, but who's heart was filled with all the love and kindness that his lacked. Mairi, since the moment she was born, had been full of laughter and joy. And she took particular joy in the moon festival and the visit from the selkies. As the Moon Maiden—for so she had been crowned each month since the beginning of her own moon cycle—she danced and she sang and she feasted with each of the guests during the festival. But she had one in particular for whom she waited, patiently or not, each month to see again.

Rona also waited less than patiently for each moon to grow into fruition and for the day of the festival to arrive. She could not visit the humans outside of the festival, but she often watched the coast from a distance, hoping for a glimpse of Mairi and her long ginger hair. This particular moon festival was Rona's tenth since she had been grown enough to attend with her sisters and her aunts. Before entering the village she made sure to smooth out her long grey hair, and pluck a bunch of wild heather from the verge. Upon encountering the Moon Maiden she gave the heather as an offering of admiration and good will.

They spent many hours of that day in each other's company. They spoke of life on land and life beneath the waves. They told each other secret dreams, and came close to confessing the longing that was in both their hearts. Mairi could not easily hide her preferment of Rona to the other guests, but she did her duty by them, honored them, always with one eye on the tall dark woman with the grey hair. This festival was not like other festivals, for this festival was the first festival after Mairi's tenth moon anniversary. After the tenth year of a maiden's moon cycle she may, if she so chooses, take a partner. This is a time when other young people express their interest, knowing the Moon Maiden might invite any one of them to her bed on the evening of the Moon Festival.

But for days Mairi had been kindly acknowledging expressions of interest, already knowing who she would invite to share her hearth. When darkness fell, and other couples began to make their way towards home, Mairi approached Rona where she sat beside her sisters. Extending a hand and a wordless invitation, she waited with heart pounding for Rona's response. Rona was surprised, for she knew what this invitation meant to the humans, and she was honored at the chance to accept it. She put her hand in Mairi's and together they walked toward her home.

When Rona left the next morning and made her way towards the shore, she was incandescent with joy. And even when her joy turned to grief at the loss of her skin, she could not help the tiny blossom of hope at the thought of being able to see Mairi again.

Because her pelt was lost Rona had no choice but to wander. She walked down the coastline searching, calling to her sisters for help. But as the sun rose high in the sky she knew it was too late. Her sisters bobbed in the water at a distance, barking to her in their familiar voices, but they could not return to the land until the next moon, and she could not return to the sea without her skin. Not knowing what else to do, she returned to the village.

When Rona walked on her bare feet into the common spaces of the village there was a rustle of shock and dismay. No one had ever seen a selkie outside of the moon festival, and their shock rendered them nearly useless. Only Mairi quickly approached Rona and, wrapping her in a wool cloak, drew her into her home and sat her before the fire. When she had heard what happened she wept as well, her tender heart having no choice but to experience Rona's grief as her own.

As the day ended Mairi tucked Rona into her own bed and let her sleep. She knew there was nothing to be done until the pelt could be found, but had no idea where to even start looking. She dozed off in front of the hearth fire, and her dreams were full of darkness and keening voices.

As the days went by, Rona remained a guest in Mairi's home, and each of the villagers came to pay their respects. The smaller children were sent to search the fields and the farmyard for the pelt, and the older ones to look along the rocky shores. But as days turned into weeks with no sign of the skin, the search became less frantic and eventually faded into a token effort and then to nothing. No one thought to ask Malcolm, or his other boys, why they would not help in the search. Malcolm was reticent when it came to any manual labor, and no one liked to press him for fear of retaliation.

The next moon festival came, and a new Moon Maiden was chosen. As the selkies entered the village from the sea they each greeted Rona with arms wide and tears in their eyes. There had been as much searching below the water as there had been above, but with no sign of her selkie skin. The festival continued, but in every heart there was a tinge of fear, and the joyous celebration was shadowed by a lurking dread.

Another month passed, and then another, and soon Rona had been living in the village for a full season. She had moments of joy, but she never forgot the search for her skin or the sea she had been forced to abandon. Each month she was visited by her sisters, who mourned her exile from their watery home. She and Mairi spent happy days together, but Mairi knew that Rona could not be truly happy when half of her world was lost to her.

Soon one season turned into two, into five, until eight full seasons had gone by with Rona living in vague contentment amongst the villagers. She and Mairi each gave birth to a daughter, one with fiery ginger hair, the other with hair the color of silver. Their family was happy, but always there was a touch of gloom upon them.

Now, all these years Malcolm had thought himself immensely clever for the trick he had played. He had hidden the seal skin in the eves of his house, and there it lived in silent melancholy until one day it came time to re-thatch the roof. Malcolm, still adverse to manual labour, hired another man from the village to do the work for him. This was a man who thatched a beautiful roof, who's wife made a beautiful loaf of bread, and who's heart was full of regret for the trick that he knew Malcolm had played. The trick he himself had been too afraid to confess for all these years.

As he thatched the roof he saw Malcolm sleeping with his feet upon the hearth. He knew that Malcolm slept with a might snore, and would not hear if another man were knocking at his door. So this man thatched the roof in peace for several hours, until he came to the spot above the open door. There, as he removed the old thatch, he noticed something tucked into the crossbeams of the roof. As he reached out to pull it loose he recognized the sleek grey color of Rona's hair. As his fingers brushed against the pelt he felt its terror and grief deep in his soul. Tears streamed down his face without warning, and he clutched the skin to his chest.

The thatcher of roofs did not fall from his ladder, but it was a close call as he slid down and sprinted towards Rona and Mairi's home. When he arrived the women opened the door to a trembling, weeping human with something silver grey cradled against his chest. He fell across

the threshold, and in a mess of words and weeping confessed to the crime of cowardice. On his knees he offered the skin to Rona, who accepted it in bewildered anticipation. As her fingers closed around the skin her knees went weak.

For the first time in eight years, she felt whole again.

Mairi caught Rona as she stumbled, and their daughters hastened to bring a stool for her to sit on. Rona sank onto the seat and wept into the skin, her salty tears bringing the pelt back to shimmering life. She could smell the salt of the sea, and feel the weight of the water around her as she breathed in its scent, her scent. Almost without knowing what she did, Rona stood from the stool and tripped out of the house. Mairi and her daughters rushed to follow, but by the time they reached the door Rona had begun to run. She loped through the village on longs legs, Mairi and the girls trailing behind her.

She ran on instinct, knowing only that there was a deep aching in the center of her chest that would never be lifted on land. She staggered down the rocks towards the sea, tore off her dress and began to pull the skin over her body. As she did she heard footsteps above her, and just as the transformation was complete she glanced up to see her human family watching her from the edge of the rocky beach. In a blink she was once more a powerful grey seal, who slipped into the cold waters of the sea and was gone.

Mairi stood on the rocks, a daughter on each side, and watched as the woman she loved disappeared beneath the waves. In a powerful fury fueled by pain and grief she marched back toward the village and her brother's house.

The thatch was still unfinished, and Malcolm was still asleep in front of the fire when she arrived. In a blaze of rage she shouted for him to wake and face her. Her hair flew out from her head as in a powerful wind, and Malcolm jumped up, startled out of his sleep. He nearly fell to his knees at the sight of her, but instead clutched the back of his chair, maneuvering it between him and her rage. He knew that he had been found out. He did not know how, but he knew at the sight of Mairi's blazing eyes and the wind whipping up around her that she knew what he had done. In her rage Mairi had no words. She felt her skin turn hot and her hair fill with static. She stared at her brother and for the first time saw him for the petty, slimy creature that he was. She opened her mouth and released a wailing howl. She filled it with her pain and anger and grief at losing her love. She also filled it with Rona's melancholy and terror, and her grief at losing the sea and the family she had grown up with. The wail echoed across the island, into the corners of every home, into the hearts of every villager, and out across the water to the swiftly disappearing selkie. When the echoes of the howl finally faded away, Malcolm was nowhere to be seen. Mairi collapsed in tears, and as one daughter with ginger hair comforted their mother, the other stepped into

Malcolm's cottage and around the empty chair. There, lying on the rug, was a large silvery- green cod fish. It flapped its tail and its mouth gapped for air. As her mother sat weeping, the young girl with silver-grey hair picked up the fish that used to be her wicked uncle Malcolm and

carried it down to the sea. There, standing upon the rocks, she drew her arm back and threw the fish as far as she could. As it flew into the air, she saw several dark grey heads bobbing above the waves. The fish splashed into the water and vanished, and the grey heads soon followed.

As the next moon festival approached, the first since Rona had left, Mairi woke early and stepped out into the village. She walked to the beach, standing on the rocky headland looking out into the sea. She thought she spotted several dark heads amongst the choppy waves, but as she waited she saw none of them approach the shore. She waited all day long, but other than the faint echo of barking across the waves, there was no sign of a single selkie.

The villagers, somewhat hesitantly for it seemed cruel to celebrate in the face of such tragedy, had prepared the festival as they usually would, but when no one arrived they became nervous. All that day the village was quiet and subdued, and when the fire was lit that evening there was no dancing and no music. A sacred trust had been broken, and the village knew they would suffer the outcome for years to come.

Some of the men of the village talked of going after Malcolm, finding him and making an example. No one outside of Mairi and her daughters knew what had happened to him. The villagers believed he had run off after the man who thatched roofs had confessed. Mairi let them believe this, knowing the truth would only bring more confusion and fear.

The next month the villagers halfheartedly prepared the festival again, and again Mairi went to the rocky edge to watch for the selkies, and again no one appeared. After the third and fourth festival in which the villagers received no guests, the preparations became less elaborate, and the celebration less formal. After the sixth and seventh months of no festival, the village stopped preparing the decorations, and the feast became a simple affair. By the ninth month of this abbreviated festival all that was left was a shared meal, a bonfire, and the song and dance that was their way of life.

During all these long months, and the many years that followed, Mairi never stopped walking out to the headland and waiting for the selkies to return. She sat all day watching the sea, hoping for one more day, one more dance. She often caught sight of a familiar grey head bobbing in the water, always watching from a distance. When her daughters came to fetch her at the end of the day she wept the entire way home.

The selkies never did return to the village, and even the seals retreated from the island. But still, ever month as the moon rises and the sun falls, you can see the bobbing heads of large seals waiting off the edge of the coast and hear the faint echoes of their voices across the water.

When I Was a Girl
by Ariel Kusby

when I was a girl I dreamed of being a fisherwoman

of casting deep nets like spells   pulling up condensations of blue
at swim team my flip turns were fastest   always forgetting
to breathe first   after practice I'd pull off my cap and sink
grew out my hair long   for this moment only   for the fanning out

in dreams I'd breast stroke   across the channel in a cage
sometimes I was a shark   eventually reaching land
becoming sea foam   always afraid of missing out   on something bluer

there are whole nights   I spend in the tub
gestating in a porcelain whale's womb   it doesn't matter
what holds the water   as long as the water holds me
I extend this allowance to velvet   to lapis
and to my own blood   which fills my skin just right
a red tide perfectly timed   the best I can do

Being Me
by Emma Jardine

Under the sea

Is where you'll find me

I swim around coral

Vibrant and floral

I bob near the surface

And gaze at the surfers

Or dive after whales

And dream of their tails

Under the sea

That's where I'll be

Dipping and diving

And glad I'm still me

Bios

AJD
AJD had this dream for a few years after getting out of the navy. Now they dream of missed city buses, tsunamis, and endless aisles of books.

Alec Ballweg
Alec doesn't know why she writes. She writes the stories that she feels need to be told (she thinks). She likes books and words and working at Powell's. But she also likes climbing and eating good food and snuggling because she's not a total nerd.

Alice
Alice can fly. She is a teacher in Nanjing, China, but she is from Chengdu. I climbed the mountain once in Chengdu. We started at six o'clock at reached the monastery after midnight. The monastarey was closed. All the inns were closed. We found one full of ghosts (we knew because, when they turned our backs to us, they disappeared) and when they turned around again to face us, show us the beds, the beds were wet and black with mold. We ran from the ghosts and in the morning met monkeys living on the mountain.

Michael Calkins
Michael Calkins has worked in bookstores for 31 years, the last 28 at Powell's.

Mickey Collins
~~Mickey rights wrongs. Mickey wrongs rites.~~ Mickey writes words, sometimes wrong words but he tries to get it write.

Robert Eversmann
Robert Eversmann used to sell books at Powell's City of Books. He is an English teacher and developmental editor. His website is roberteversmann. com

Desmond Everest Fuller
My name is Desmond Everest Fuller. My fiction has appeared in Rasasvada Creative and the Gorge Literary Review. I live and work in Portland, Oregon. I did work for years off and on in the fantastic bookstore, Artifacts: Good Books and Bad Art in Hood River, Oregon.

Emma Jardine
Emma Jardine is from Belfast, Ireland. She is an English teacher in Nanjing, China, where she manages the children's library.

Monika Kawiak
I was born in 1982 in Gdynia, a Polish town that is said to have been built "from the dreams and sea". After graduating from the University in Gdansk (specialization in History) I mostly worked as a Managing Editor for a publishing house. I have moved to Portland in October 2017, just in time to help as a volunteer at the Portland Book Festival. My life in a new city has been connected with books ever since. Luckily for me, at the beginning of summer 2018, I became a part of the Inventory team at Powell's. I spend my free time reading or admiring Pacific Northwest's nature, and, from time to time, trying to write my Polish thoughts using English words.

Benjamin Kessler
Benjamin Kessler's writing has appeared in National Geographic, Pom Pom Lit Mag, Superstition Review, Hobart, and Portland Review. He reads for The Masters Review and lives in Portland, Oregon where he works at Powell's City of Books.

Ariel Kusby
Ariel Kusby is a writer and bookseller based in Portland, Oregon. She currently works in the Rose and Orange rooms at Powell's City of Books, where she pays special attention to children's books about witches, odd cookbooks, and gnome gardening guides. You can check out her writing at www.arielkusby.com.

Sarah McCleod-Martinez
Sarah "Kitty" McLeod-Martinez is an artist who can usually be found where she works: Powell's City of Books in Portland, Oregon. When she's not there or arting, she is probably hanging out with her wife or girlfriend, or trying to figure out which cord her cat has recently chewed through. If you ask her to read your cards, she will likely pour you a stiff drink. You can find more of her art on Instagram: @arsenikitty.

Maya McOmie
Maya is a poet, performer and daydreamer who probably spends too much time thinking about snacks. She grew up with two languages and cultures and her poetry and art attempts to process the complex emotions that are part of being a person. She works in a bookstore where, to much joy and chagrin, she finds at least ten things she wants to read every day.

Azalea Micketti
Azalea Micketti is a writer, director, and bookseller who is passionate about storytelling and sharing books. She grew up in Ashland, OR and has lived in her (second) favorite city for almost nine months. She works at Powell's City of Books as a bookseller.

Leanna Moxley
Leanna Moxley spends most of her time wandering in and out of fictional dimensions, often guiding others through these portals in her work as a Powell's bookseller, and sometimes as a college writing teacher.

Elizabeth Neal
Elizabeth Neal is a Portland actress and bookseller. She is proud of her Union, ILWU Local 5.

Oaktea
Oaktea has always been in love with every aspect of a book--from the design to its contents, everything contributes to the experience. She started making comics for the all-in-one art and words combination, and eventually started working in bookstores to feed her voracious habit, as well as her love and respect for the form of the book itself.

Timothy Arliss O'Brien
I am an interdisciplinary artist in music composition, writing, and visual arts. My goal is to connect people to accessible new compositions that showcase virtuosic abilities without losing touch of realistic emotions and virtue. I also want to produce writing that connects the reader to themselves in a way that promotes wonder and self realization. I would also like to create visual art demanding of the senses that thrusts people into a new world and a new perspective. Check out more of my music and publications at www.timothyarlissobrien.com.

Mike Santiago
Michael Santiago is an aspiring author and current English teacher in Nanjing, China. He decided to get into education so that he could not only travel the world doing what he loves, but to ignite that creative spark by putting the power of storytelling into the hands of his students. His creative drive and passion for literature has helped him translate the power of books and their capacity to bestow knowledge onto his children.

BEN TALLEY

Ben Talley was raised in the humid stew of Alabama and is a pretty okay guy, despite what the cat thinks. If you speak to his grandmother, let her know that he eats regularly.

ERIC THRALBY

Captain by trade, Cpt. Eric Thralby works wood in his long off-days. He time-to-time pilots the Bremerton Ferry (Bremerton—Vashon; Vahon—Bremerton), while other times sells books on amazon.com, SellerID: plainpages. He'll sell any books the people love, strolling down to library and yard sales, but he loves especially books of Romantic fiction, not of risqué gargoyles, not harlequin romance, but knights, errant or of the Table. Eric has not published before, but has read in local readings at the Gig Harbor Candy Company and the Lavender Inne, also in Gig Harbor.

JONATHAN VAN BELLE

Jonathan van Belle is a bookseller at Powell's. He's the author of three books, including the pre-posthumously published *Charter Party Companion to Private Holidays* (all available in the most spider-infested kudzu undergrowth of Amazon). At the moment, Jonathan is working to build a philosophical community in Portland, with the aim of establishing a permanent residence for the *Portland Philosophy Museum*.

GEOFF WALLACE

Geoff Wallace is a 55-year-old trapped in the body of an 18-year-old. His twin selves are at work on many projects at once. He likes shelving picture books at Powell's in Portland, Oregon.

Z.B. WAGMAN

Z.B. Wagman has found work amongst the stacks in libraries and bookstores. He can currently be found at Powell's City of Books looking after all of his childhood favorites in the Rose room.